A BRIDE FOR THE COWBOY

LINDA GOODNIGHT

CHAPTER 1

*P*repare yourself.

The ominous words hissed inside Ace Caldwell's head like a pair of vipers.

He'd wrestled with the warning all night and again on the long drive from the Triple C Ranch to the Tulsa private investigator's waiting room.

Prepare himself? How? For what? The news couldn't get any worse. Could it?

What was the woman going to do? Slice out his black heart? Run over him with her red Toyota? Either of which he deserved and some of which she'd threatened at the time, but Marisa Foreman wasn't the murdering type. Or she hadn't been.

Her brother, on the other hand, should have shot him on sight. If he'd been able.

Ace heaved a long, agitated gust of air and raked a hand over his clean-shaven face. He stuck a finger beneath the hated tie and tugged. Why did he dress up in the first place? This wasn't a funeral. He hoped.

Normally a confident guy, Ace hadn't been this nervous since his first AA meeting in the basement of the Clay City Baptist Church. *Church.* A place that still made him a little antsy, as if he didn't belong there and never would. He rubbed sweaty palms over the knees of his jeans.

Making recompense for past sins was harder than he'd ever imagined, and he had plenty to repay. Especially this time.

Forgiveness might be as free as Preacher Marcus claimed, but redemption was another matter. Redemption came with a high price tag and a hearty dose of sticker shock. Ace knew this for a fact, an agonizing, belly-crawling fact. But crawl he would if that's what it took.

For what must have been the hundredth time, Ace pushed up from the cushy waiting-room chair and stalked to the receptionist's desk.

"My appointment was at ten-thirty." His throat was a load of gravel stirred by a swarm of angry hornets.

"I'm sorry, Mr. Caldwell. The first client is taking longer than expected." She forced a smile, her brown lipstick stretching to a near grimace. And who wouldn't be a tad touchy by now? He'd nagged her for an hour, growing more agitated and cranky by the ask. "You're welcome to have some coffee or tea while you wait."

He didn't want coffee or tea. He wanted a shot of tequila.

The thought came out of nowhere and caught him off guard. He was normally pretty good at handling those random, fiery darts that shot through his brain and unloaded their poisonous temptations.

He did *not* want a shot of tequila, thank you very much. He wanted to talk to the private investigator, find out Marissa's contact information, and resolve the *prepare yourself* comment.

He already knew the mine field that lay ahead when he found Marisa. She hated him, and for good reason. What he'd done to her brother was unforgivable.

Ace squeezed his eyes tight for two seconds and tried to erase the sudden, searing memory. If he thought about Chance too much, he'd be tempted for more than a shot. He'd want the whole bottle.

Mustering his sweet side—the one Connie said was natural, though he'd come to doubt he had a sweet bone in his athletic body—he leaned an elbow on the short counter between him and the receptionist. Nice was important. He didn't need to add another person to his long list of Step-Nine apologies.

"Sorry. Not your fault." He forced a smile, tried for crooked and charming, and settled for adequate. "Maybe I'll have some coffee, after all. Thanks."

Without waiting for the effect of his lackluster charm, Ace spun toward the credenza at one end of the waiting area. A Keurig offered options and, with a quick glance around to be sure no one was watching, he chose chamomile tea. The bunkhouse boys would have a field day if they knew the big boss of The Triple C Ranch was sipping girly tea. Even if someone held a cattle prod to his eyeballs, he'd never admit it, but the stuff calmed his jitters. If he drank any more coffee today, he'd be climbing the walls.

The tea trickled into the cup, making splashy sounds, and the pot gurgled. Antsy as an Alabama sugar bowl in summer, he tapped his fingers on top of the credenza until, at ever-loving last, the pot coughed into silence.

Foam cup cradled in his hands as if someone would, any minute, point and accuse him of drinking wimpy tea, Ace sipped the brew, took a deep breath, and blew it out. Slow and easy. *Calm yourself.*

"Mr. Caldwell, Mr. Buckley will see you now." The receptionist shot him a relieved glance.

Ace sipped once more, tossed the remaining tea in the trash, and stalked into an office off the waiting area. Not much more than a desk and a computer, the room was small, but the man in the big leather chair wasn't. At least six-six with the bulk to match, Jon Buckley would have a hard time doing anything without being noticed. But after years on the Tulsa police force, he managed to be an effective private investigator. In a dress shirt, no tie, with his jacket draped over the back of the chair, he swiveled away from the computer to face Ace.

The man stood, and Ace, who boasted six feet in socks, felt dwarfed.

"Just checking my stocks," Buckley said.

The men exchanged handshakes.

"Nasdaq's up." As CEO of a major spread like The Triple C, Ace kept an eagle eye on their investments. Cattle markets weren't the only thing this cowboy invested in.

"Yeah. Looking good lately." The PI motioned toward a chair. "Sit. Relax."

"Easy for you to say." But he sat anyway.

"Well, then, I'll cut to the chase. You're not paying me to be your broker." Jon offered a self-satisfied grunt as he settled back into his chair. The leather groaned. "As I told you on the phone the day of your brother's wedding, we found her. The surprise is she was easy to locate. She's in Clay City."

"No way." Clay City was less than fifteen miles from Calypso and The Triple C. "I checked her old place a couple months back. Someone else lives there, and the neighbors had no idea where she'd gone or when she'd return."

He'd also phoned her old cell number, only to discover she'd changed it. Probably because of him.

"She's back now. Different address, but she's there."

Ace gripped the chair arms and leaned forward. "Where has she been? Is she okay? Where's Chance? How's he doing?"

He had a hundred questions, most of which only Marisa could answer.

The PI scooted a manila file folder across the tidy desk. "Everything we learned is in here, but the upshot is this. Shortly after he was stabilized at St. Francis, Marisa moved Chance to an out-of-state rehab facility that works specifically with spinal cord injuries. They released him a few weeks ago."

Hope spurted like the original Spindletop oil well. Chance had been released. "So if they're back in Clay City, the rehab must have helped. Is he on his feet again?"

God, please let the answer be yes. Let Chance be the strong, athletic man he was before the accident.

"After eighteen months of therapy, he stopped making progress. He's in a care center in Clay City."

Hope took a death spiral.

"Care center? As in a nursing home?" Though not unexpected, the news slammed Ace in the gut with more force than a mule's kick. Hadn't he hoped? Hadn't he prayed? And hadn't he procrastinated finding Marisa because he feared exactly this?

"Marisa works there. From the financials I ran, they're wallowing in debt, and she's working two jobs to keep her head above water. The medical bills are astronomical."

"I paid the bills in Tulsa." Ace swiped a hand over his face. "Then I lost track and... Can you get me that information?"

"She won't let you."

"She can't stop me. She needs the money, and I have it. Or can get it. She blames me for Chance's injury, and I owe her. Get me that information."

"Will do. But don't say I didn't warn you."

"Right." As if he would. He knew how independent and determined Marisa could be, traits he'd once admired that now frustrated him and had since the day she'd offered him a police escort out of St. Francis Hospital.

Not his most shining moment.

Eager to do what had to be done, Ace shoved out of the chair, grabbed the folder, and headed toward the door. Get it over with and put this horrible episode behind him. Except Chance couldn't. Not ever.

"Ace. Wait. There's something else."

Ace paused at the door to glance over one shoulder. This must be the *prepare yourself* part.

"Miss Foreman has asked that out of respect and decency—her words, not mine—you do not contact her. She doesn't want to see you. In fact, she was furious I had tracked her down and even threatened to move again. She can't afford to, but she might do it anyway. She was that upset."

All the energy drained from Ace. Since the last day at the hospital, she'd avoided him, hid from him, hated him. And rightfully so. He'd paralyzed her brother. Drunk and stupid, the man who'd claimed to love her had betrayed her in a way that would haunt them all the rest of their lives.

With one curt nod, Ace stalked out of the office.

Marisa didn't want to see him. No surprise in that, only a sharp, hot pain. Some days he struggled to look in the mirror and see himself.

Stewing, half-praying, though he wondered if either did any good, Ace climbed in his truck and leaned his arms on the steering wheel until his heart quit pounding and the blood in his temples settled into a low swoosh instead of a Niagara-Falls roar.

A man with as many sins as he had compiled in thirty-six years would spend the rest of his life making things right. Step nine was a long and seemingly never ending list of failures, of wrongs against decent people. All in the name of a good time that wasn't so good, after all.

Facing the people he'd hurt was the hardest part. People like Marisa. Like Chance. But face them he would. It was the only way to defeat the demon living inside him.

The one that said a bottle of tequila would cure every-thing. It wouldn't. God knew he'd tried after the accident. If not for family—Nate and Emily, Connie and Gilbert—he might have drunk himself to death.

Thanks to them and to God, he'd crawled out of his despair and gotten sober. Fifteen months and counting. And he'd never go back. *Never.* The cost was too high.

One way or the other, he would see Marisa. He would see for himself the damage he'd done to her and to her brother. This time he'd be sober. He'd face his guilt head on, and somehow he would find a way to make amends.

With a determined huff, he fumbled in the console for a cinnamon candy, popped it in his mouth, and cranked the engine on his big diesel truck. Then, fighting a serious case of shakes, he headed toward the interstate and the woman who never wanted to see him again.

MARISA SCRAPED her hair into a tight ponytail and secured it with four twists of a pink hair band. She stuck an extra band in the pocket of her scrubs, along with a pen, a tube of Chapstick and her prepaid cell phone. She glanced at her watch, a cheap twelve-dollar device that worked fine for her purposes. She wasn't picky. Couldn't afford to be.

Forty-five minutes until she had to be at work. For once, she might have time to eat something before her shift. She straightened the items on the small vanity and reorganized the overhead medicine cabinet again. Confident the tiny bathroom was neat and she wouldn't come home exhausted to a mess, she headed into the kitchen. Last night's pasta salad sounded good.

She took the bowl from the fridge just as a knock sounded at the door. Since bringing Chance back to Clay City, the neighbors had proved friendly, occasionally appearing on her step with food or an offer for their church group to visit her brother at the Care Center. The latter she refused for now. Chance was in no mood to see anyone. He was mad at God, mad at the world. She'd thought bringing him home to the familiar would help, but if anything, his depression seemed worse.

She didn't know what do for him anymore. She prayed, she worked, and she tried to stay positive. But positive was hard to find these days.

The neighbors, however, cheered her, and she was thankful to have found a safe neighborhood of older people and aging homes like hers where the rent was reasonable. Last week, Mr. Sims, the elder gentleman in the other side of the duplex, mowed her lawn while she was at work. She'd repaid him with a plate of oatmeal cookies and an afternoon listening to stories of his late wife. He was a nice man, but lonely.

Smiling and expecting to see his wrinkled, friendly face, she went to open the front door.

A shock wave reverberated through her body and crash landed at her feet. She wished the sky would open and a UFO would suck her into the clouds.

Ace Caldwell. The man she'd prayed to forget and to forgive lest she lose her own soul in hating him stood on her stoop, looking handsomer than ever.

That was just wrong.

She slammed the door in his green-eyed face.

The knocking recommenced, harder this time. "Marisa, I only want to talk to you."

Marisa leaned her back against the door and fought not to slide to the hardwood. Sweat broke out. She clenched her fist and her teeth. She hated him, hated him, *hated* him.

"Marisa, please. Open the door." He knocked harder and raised his voice.

Really? Just like that he thought he could show up at her door and be welcomed in with a big, cheery smile. Not in this lifetime.

Furious, she turned her face to the wood and shouted, "Go away and never come back."

He didn't.

Instead, he must have use both fists, and the knocks grew louder. He pounded. Banged. And he yelled. Loud enough that deaf Mrs. Francis at the end of block would hear him. "I'm not leaving until we talk. So you might as well open the door."

His voice elevated with each word. And the door quivered from his incessant pounding. If he kept that up, he'd disturb the entire neighborhood, older neighbors who treasured peace and quiet. Maybe they'd blame her, think she had a wild boyfriend.

The thought should have been funny, but it wasn't. She'd had a wild boyfriend. Two years ago. Ace Caldwell. A wild and fun cowboy with a party attitude.

He hollered louder, punctuating each word with a hammering fist.

He was still a wild man. Probably drunk. And still everything she could not have in her life.

"I'm not leaving, Marisa!"

Oh, yes he was.

She yanked the door open. If eyes were bullets, she hoped hers were firing on all cylinders. AK-47s.

"What are you doing here?" Teeth tight, she forced the words. "You are not welcome. I don't want to talk to you or see you. I told that to the man you had following me. Which is a violation of my privacy, by the way. Don't do it again."

Ace removed his gray Resistol, pretending to be a gentleman, and held it in both hands. "He was a legitimate private investigator. I had to find you."

"You found me. Now leave."

"Not until we talk."

Marisa's lip curled. "You must be drunk. As usual."

The man with the perennial tan blanched a sickly beige. "I don't do that anymore."

She laughed, a bitter sound even to her own ears. "Or any less, I imagine."

Had she ever once been with him that he hadn't smelled like alcohol?

The Holy Spirit tapped at her conscience. She wasn't acting much like a Christian, but then, she never had around Ace. He'd led her down the wrong path, and she'd followed like a hungry puppy in order to be with him. The things she'd done in the name of love shamed her even now. She'd loved him, and her adoration had cost her brother his mobility.

"I want to help him." He twisted the hat until she thought he'd rip it in half. "And you."

"We don't need your help."

11

"Yes, you do."

She bristled. The truth, spoken with soft words, only upset her more.

If any human could grow porcupine quills, she thought she might be the one. "You paid the hospital bill against my will. I tried to reject it, but the hospital refused to let me."

"I know." His voice was soft, wounded. She wouldn't fall for his pitiful act of contrition. "I wanted to help then. I want to help now. Any way I can."

"I don't want your money." Blood money. That's what it was. He was trying to buy his way to redemption. "Neither of us do."

"How is he?"

"How do you *think* he is?" Bitterness welled in her throat, spilled out between her tight lips. "An athlete with so much potential. New in his career but happy and successful. A young man who thought you hung the moon." Like her. She'd thought the same, and she'd been so weak that even after the accident, she'd wanted Ace to hold her and tell her everything would be fine. But it wasn't fine. It never would be.

"I want to see him."

"No." She started to shut the door again.

He stuck his boot toe inside. "I'm trying to make amends, Marisa."

"Amends? *Amends?*" Her voice rose on each word. She leaned forward, livid now. "There are some things money can't buy. Take legs for instance. Can you buy Chance new legs? Can you reconnect his spinal cord?"

The cruel words hit their mark. He stumbled back,

head down, shoulders slumped, his hat dangling at his side.

Marisa slammed the door, expecting to feel better, vindicated. If the rattling in her chest was any indication, she felt worse. Way worse.

One eye to the peephole, she watched the cowboy. He'd stepped off the square piece of concrete she called a porch and stood in the sunlight, sculpted jaw still pointed toward her door, the temples of his black hair surprisingly shot with gray. He was only in his thirties. How could he be turning gray?

Finally, he replaced the cowboy hat, stared for another second or two as if contemplating another knock, then turned away and walked slowly to his big, fancy pickup truck.

Rich cowboy who thought money could solve everything. It couldn't, though God knew, she needed more of it than she could make at two entry-level jobs.

"Oh, Lord, what am I supposed to do now? You know how bad he is for me, for Chance. Why did he have to come here?"

Anxiety tightened her shoulders to the point of fracture. In search of calm, she straightened the pictures on the wall. She and her brother at Chance's college graduation. The other of Chance in his first coaching job, surrounded by his baseball team. She'd been as proud as a parent. All her years of hard work to get him through school and then through college had finally paid off.

And then she'd introduced her precious brother to her boyfriend.

Ace Caldwell had been the love of her life. Or so she'd

thought. But in the end, he'd been part of the twisted psychological pattern she'd promised never to fall victim to. A child of alcoholics falling for a man heading in that direction as fast he could go.

Her fault. Her fault. Her fault. She could blame Ace all day long, but she was guilty too. After protecting her younger brother all his life, she'd handed him over to disaster.

Appetite gone, she went into the kitchen and put the bowl of pasta back in the fridge, pausing to reorganize the condiments into alphabetical order.

She'd sworn to never date a man who so much as drank a beer. And what had she done? One nod from that handsome cowboy, and she'd tumbled like an Olympic gymnast. Never mind that he'd been leading her brother down the wrong path and her as well. She'd fallen for him, loved him wildly, and paid for her sins with her brother's future.

CHAPTER 2

*H*e deserved Marisa's vitriolic tirade. Ace knew that. Just as he knew he couldn't expect her to fall all over him in forgiveness. But seeing her, experiencing her anger and pain all over again, tore him apart. He'd hoped, prayed, that she'd healed, that she didn't hate him and wasn't still hurting. Another unanswered prayer.

If his heart hadn't already been shredded worse than a box of government documents, it would be now. But if absolution came from being shredded, beaten, stomped, he'd take anything Marisa had to dish out.

Ace sat inside his truck sucking on a cinnamon disk while he reread the file folder, searching for the name of Chance's care center. Chance was an adult, not her minor child, and Ace was going to see him whether Marisa liked it or not. The man deserved no less than a face-to-face apology.

He found the entry, touched it with one finger. Sunset Manor. The name gave him the willies. Sunset, as if the sun was going down permanently on everyone in the place.

Not Chance. Please God, not Chance.

Though Ace was ten years older, he and Marisa's brother had hit it off from the start. They'd shared a love for the outdoors, for all things sports and athletic. He'd taught Chance to ride horses. Chance had taught him the finer points of throwing a curveball. They'd both enjoyed fishing. And they'd had a blast.

Until Chance's twenty-fourth birthday.

Squeezing a hand over his mouth so he wouldn't bawl like a two-year-old, Ace punched the address into his navigation system and followed the voice to a long, low-brick building.

The front of Sunset Manor was cheery with blooming rose shrubs, and the small lawn had been recently mowed. The back and sides were surrounded by a tall wooden privacy fence.

Was Chance sitting behind that wall in the sunshine, legs useless, wishing he was at a ballgame or fishing in one of Ace's forty ponds? Didn't Marisa understand? Ace could make those things happen. He could take Chance places, do guy things with him.

Or was Chance bedfast, helpless, unable to do anything at all? He'd been on the ventilator at first. Was he still?

Ace didn't know, and the not knowing scared him as he parked and walked to the entryway. Through the glass, he saw a half dozen senior residents, most in wheelchairs, and most asleep. A sprightly lady in a vibrant pink duster

scooted her walker right past the door without acknowl-
edging him.

The door was locked, a security keypad to his left, but
he didn't know the code. He knocked on the glass.

A hefty woman in maroon scrubs and a nametag
appeared from the dimness, pushed the inside handle, and
leaned around the door. "Can I help you?"

"I'd like to visit Chance Foreman."

Her forehead wrinkled like folded bread dough. "Who?"

"Chance Foreman. I'm told he's a patient here."

"Sorry, hon. You must have the wrong facility. Try the
others in town. If not there, he might be over in Rock
Springs." She pulled the door shut with a snap and a click
and waddled away.

Puzzled, Ace returned to his truck to check the facility's name and address. The big sign next to the street
proclaimed this building to be Sunset Manor. Could there
be another one? Maybe a Sunset One and a Sunset Two?

He located the PI's number and tapped the keypad.
The receptionist who didn't like him much answered. He
identified himself and asked for Jon.

"Mr. Buckley is out for the rest of the day, Mr. Caldwell. Call back in the morning."

After hanging up, Ace tried another tactic. He entered,
"nursing homes" into his Garmin, and the navigator
returned three names and addresses in Clay City, one of
which was Sunset Manor. He tapped the first of the two
he'd yet to visit and pointed the truck in that direction.

Clay City wasn't huge, and in less than thirty minutes,
Ace concluded that either he'd been lied to by someone or

Chance did not reside in any of the three care facilities in Clay City. Figuring lies were the most likely, considering Marisa's animosity, and with his patience running thin, he drove back through town to Sunset Manor.

As he pulled into the parking lot, a familiar figure exited an older model red Corolla. The car looked familiar too. The same one she'd driven two years ago.

He'd been duped all right.

"Marisa." He wanted to be mad at her, but he couldn't muster the energy, and the truth was, he had no right. She, on the other hand, had every right.

She was still as pretty as a bouquet of flowers, and he experienced a twist in his chest at the sight of her. Even with a perky, brunette ponytail swaying against her shoulders, she looked worn down and exhausted. She was also a good ten or fifteen pounds lighter than she'd been two years ago. And she'd never been anywhere near heavy.

What had she been through in the past eighteen months? A living hell, he supposed, though he was unable to fathom the stress, the fear, the worry. Chance had been her whole world until Ace had come along. She'd raised her brother, taking him out of foster care when she'd turned eighteen and Chance was eleven. She'd fought valiantly to put him through school, to give him a better life.

When Ace had learned about her crazy childhood and how she'd battled to keep custody of her little brother, his admiration had known no bounds. Independent, strong, devoted. That was his Marisa.

From her reaction to his offer of financial assistance, she was still all those qualities. But she'd been vulnerable, too. Eager for someone strong in her life, someone she could lean on and love.

And he'd betrayed her with his bad-boy behavior.

Contrite, grieved, he prayed as he guided his truck into the parking spot next to hers. Praying for the words to say, for understanding, and for a calm he didn't feel, Ace hopped out before she could spot him and rush into the locked confines of the nursing home.

He knew the minute she saw him. She paused, stiffened, and her once smiling mouth thinned to the point of disappearing.

Ace held out a hand, pleading. "Don't go. Please."

Her eyes, dark gray and sad, studied him as if he were a specimen she'd hoped wouldn't grow on her Petri dish. "You always had trouble taking no for an answer."

"I'm sorry about that. Sorry about so many things." He held her gaze, though he was afraid of what he'd find there and let his own sorrow and grief pour out. Now might be his only chance. "I know you hate me. You have every right. But I need for you to know that I regret everything and anything I did that hurt you."

She clutched a Walmart sack in one hand, crinkling it with the pressure. She didn't reply. But she didn't bolt either.

"I don't expect forgiveness," Ace went on, encouraged, "but I'd like to help you in whatever way I can, anything you decide is appropriate."

"The best thing you can do is to leave us alone."

He chewed on that, found it too bitter to swallow and rejected it. "Remember all those times I teased you about being a Christian, about taking your faith too far? I was wrong. Faith is the only thing holding me together these days. I suspect the same is true for you."

Though wary and watchful still, something shifted in Marisa's demeanor. She relaxed. Not a lot, but enough that he knew that she was listening and wouldn't run away. For now.

She glanced at a large-faced watch on her wrist. "I have to be on duty in ten minutes."

That wasn't long enough. He had so much to tell her and so many words backed up inside him like a clogged pipe. He needed her to know about AA, about the changes he was making, the ones God was making in him, and he had to learn about Chance.

"Ten minutes then." He could ask for more later.

He stepped closer. Her eyes widened, but she didn't back away. She wasn't afraid of him. She just loathed what he stood for.

"Why are you doing this, Ace? Why couldn't you leave us in peace? Haven't you hurt us enough?"

He had. The sharp, jagged slice of that truth lacerated his very soul. But that's why he was here.

One look through the deep windows to her soul, and he was torn between falling at her feet and pulling her into his arms. He wanted to touch her so badly, he could barely breathe. To hold her and promise not to ever let anything hurt her again. But he'd been her greatest source of pain. How did he protect her from himself when he couldn't leave her alone any more than he could ever take another drink? He required her forgiveness the same way he required oxygen, a fact that scared him half to death.

He licked dry lips, blood pounding in his ears. He'd

have a headache later, and he'd want a drink. Stress did that to him. But he couldn't allow stress to win anymore.

Gently, praying she'd recognize his remorse, he asked, "I want to see him."

"I don't think that's a good idea, Ace." Her voice was quieter too, not so angry, and the thrumming eased in Ace's temples. "Chance is fragile. You'll upset him."

"Will you ask him? Let him make the decision?"

Another car pulled into the parking lot, and a door slammed. Marisa glanced in that direction. "I have to go in."

She started to back away, and he did the unthinkable. He reached out, wrapped his fingers around her too-thin arm. She glanced down at the place where he held her and backed up again.

Ace dropped his hold. "What time do you get off?"

"Eleven."

"Will you meet for coffee? Tell me what Chance says. Talk to me about him?" About you. But he didn't say the last. She might take it wrong, and right now they were on shaky ground. Earthquake ground.

Marisa looked away, out across a parking lot of cars, all gleaming in the sunlight. Even the dirty ones. A tiny frown creased the spot between her eyebrows. He wished he still had the right to smooth it away.

Slowly, she shook her head. "There are some things that can't be fixed. Chance is one of them. Go back to your ranch and leave us in peace."

"Marisa—"

"I'll give him your message, but don't expect to hear from me."

With a regal fling of her ponytail, Marisa walked away, leaving him right where he'd started. Guilty and broken with no way to repay his debt.

MARISA TREMBLED as she entered the care center, her mind rolling with the last few minutes. She should have run the moment she spotted his truck in the lot, but Ace had seemed different, not the same cocky cowboy who knew he was attractive and used it to his advantage. He'd been repentant and humble, two words she would never have equated with the proud ranch owner.

Didn't matter. He was who he was, and he'd done what he'd done. She wouldn't be stupid enough to be fooled by him again. In theory, forgiveness sounded easy. Doing it was a whole other universe. Someone once said there was a fine line between love and hate. She got that. Big time.

She clocked in and made her rounds, saving Chance's room for last so she could spend extra time there. Each time she came to work, the care center's smell of disinfectant and urine got to her for a few minutes until she'd acclimated, ratcheting her compassion for those who lived here permanently. As a certified nurse's aide, she'd worked in plenty of nursing homes, and only the very best managed to avoid the odor. She couldn't afford the very best.

Outside her brother's door, she paused to put on her happiest expression. She didn't want him to know how upset she'd been since Ace's appearance. He had enough worries. It was her job as the healthy one to protect him, control who came and went, decide his medical care, and make sure every order was followed. Rhonda, the RN, called her a control freak, but what did she know? Rhonda's baby brother wasn't paralyzed from the waist down.

When she pushed inside, Chance was seated in his chair, his back to her as he faced the exterior windows. Thank goodness he hadn't stayed in bed again all day. But he stared out over the parking lot. Marisa tensed. Had he seen Ace?

"Hey, brother. You're up! It's a gorgeous day out there, isn't it?" She straightened his rumpled bed as she talked, keeping her tone upbeat and cheery. "Sunshine. Blue sky. Fluffy clouds. Remember how we used to find pictures in the clouds? You were a master at finding the best ones."

Her brother didn't turn or join her falsely happy conversation. When they came, his words were low and tired. "I saw you talking to Ace."

Marisa's hands paused, sheets cool against her fingers. Her eyelids dropped shut. Chance had seen them. He'd have questions she didn't want to answer.

"I sent him away."

"How is he?"

She huffed. "Sober."

"What did he want?"

The bitterness returned. "To make amends, he said. As if he could."

"Did he want to see me?"

"He's a fool if he thinks that's going to happen. I told the nurse's desk that he is not permitted in this building. You've been hurt enough by that man."

Chance's reply was silence. Since the accident, she never knew for certain what her brother was thinking. He refused to talk much, to share his feelings or ever tell her when he was in pain. Mostly, he sat and stared into space, depressed, bitter, lonely, and refusing to cooperate in his care plan.

She rounded his chair and crouched beside him. Gently, she took his hand. "Would you like me to take you out on the patio for a while? The sun is nice and warm, not scalding hot yet."

"No."

She sighed, a long, worried breath, suffering with him. "Chance, you have to try."

"I hate it here."

Obviously. "Give it time. We've only been home a few weeks. In no time, your old friends will learn you're back, and you can reconnect. I could call some of them, if you'd like."

He turned his face toward her. Her brother was a handsome, masculine man, his blue, soulful eyes and bright smile once enough to keep his cell phone pinging constantly. Now, he rarely smiled, and he couldn't afford a cell phone.

"I don't want them to see me like this. Ace already knows. He saw me in the hospital."

An episode she didn't want to rehash. "He's the reason you're in here."

Chance lifted a hand and touched her hair. "Big sister, so fierce. You want to find him guilty and let me go free, but we both know the truth."

"He was the adult. He should have stopped you."

"I'm an adult, too. And I was then. Sometimes you forget that."

24

The hornet's nest of anger stirred to life. She leaped up, fists tight at her sides. "He should have protected you. He should have known you were in no shape to drive."

Ace Caldwell had let her baby brother drive drunk, because *he* had been too drunk to take the wheel. He'd been passed out in the backseat when Chance left the road and rolled the truck. Ace had come away unscathed except for a well-deserved hangover.

"I hate this place." Chance said, his tone tired and hopeless. "I hate being a cripple. I hate myself for being so stupid."

"It was Ace's fault. He shouldn't have taken you out partying."

Chance's mouth twisted. "Some birthday present, huh?"

The words pierced her. She was his big sister, the closest thing to a mother he could remember, but she'd failed to protect him from the man she'd loved.

Chance sighed and went silent again, broody, his gaze far away. She wondered if he thought about running and playing ball, about the athletic things he'd once done but could do no more. She was sure he did, but she was afraid to ask.

Her pager buzzed, and she kissed his forehead and left to answer the call. By the time she returned, she had her emotions under control.

When she re-entered the room, this time to urge him toward the dining area for dinner, he refused. She'd known he would. Every night, she delivered his tray to this room while he hid away, too depressed to interact. At least today he'd talked to her. He didn't always.

She wasn't giving Ace credit for that.

"I was thinking." He slowly, painstakingly wheeled his chair around to face her.

"Dangerous," she joked. "Might burn out a brain cell."

He didn't smile, and she missed the bright, positive glow he used to exude.

"All you've ever done as long as I can remember is work and take care of me."

"You're my brother. I wanted you to follow your dreams, to go to college and have the things we didn't have growing up."

"And you did it, sis. I was finally on my own. You could finally, for the first time in your life, chase your own dreams. Now you can't."

"You're the only thing that matters to me, Chance. Nothing else is important."

"Ace was. You loved him 'Risa, and he loved you."

"He loved his liquor more." But for a while, she'd thought he loved her as much as she'd loved him. She'd dreamed big, just as Chance said. And oh, the searing agony of loss, a double loss when he'd betrayed that love in such a tragic manner.

"You were happy. At long last, you had plans for *you*, for your future instead of mine. Now, you're trapped again. Only this time, forever."

"Don't think that. I'm not trapped. I'm not."

Her brother's soulful eyes said he saw right through the protests.

CHAPTER 3

There was a party going on at the Triple C Ranch. The scent of grilled steaks perfumed the expansive back lawn and patio while folks Ace considered family talked and sipped iced tea and soda pop. Later, after dinner, they'd open up the pool house for a little water fun.

Adoption day was a big event for the Caldwell family, especially for his brother, Nate, his recent bride, Whitney, and their three-year-old twins, Olivia and Sophia. Nate had always wanted family and kids. Not that he had let on or talked about it much, but Nate was born to be a family man. He adored kids, especially Whitney's little dark-eyed dolls, and they adored him in return.

Ace leaned against the patio post and watched his brother's new daughters play with Bowzer, the aging stock dog. Bowzer, tongue lolling, seemed thrilled to have new creatures to herd. An older child, Daisy, played with them, the perfect babysitter. The perky, blond nine-year-old had practically become part of the family too after her father was sent to prison.

The whole gang was here for the big celebration. Connie, the Triple C housekeeper and Ace's mother of the heart. Gilbert, his late father's best friend who'd lived and worked on the Triple C longer than Ace had been alive. Longer than any of the kids had been around. The Seminole Indian and the Mexican housekeeper were as much family as Ace's brothers and sisters.

Sister Emily was here, too, the diamond rings on her left hand almost as shiny as her green eyes whenever she glanced at her new husband, Levi Donley, or the baby boy sleeping in the stroller. Ace marveled that an infant could sleep through the Caldwell noise. He marveled too that Levi and Emily had gotten back together after years apart. Years when Emily had loved, lost and grieved more than anyone should have to, but her faith had never wavered, and God had given her Levi and the baby she'd longed for.

He couldn't say the same for his own faith. In fact, even though Connie and Dad had raised him right, and Connie had prayed over him and taken him to church, he'd never had much faith at all until after the accident.

He took a long swig of his pop, pondering life and family and his own peculiar situation.

The Triple C Ranch was alive these days in a way it hadn't been in years.

He was more alive, too, though after yesterday's fiasco with Marisa, he felt like the bottom of the barrel again.

"You didn't expect her to welcome you with open arms, did you?" Nate wielded a giant grilling fork, the lid to the huge grill flipped up so he could check the fragrant steaks.

"I knew it wouldn't be easy, but I thought she'd talk to me."

"After she nearly had you arrested last time?"

"I was drunk, Nate." Drunk and loud and obnoxious. In a hospital filled with sick people. "She had good reason."

The truth still shamed him, but his brother knew where he'd been and the struggle he'd had with alcohol. Still had. Nate might not know everything and for that, Ace was thankful, but he'd been a rock of support in the months since Ace decided to get sober. One day at a time. Some days it was one minute at a time. Days like yesterday.

"I can't let it go. She's broke, working two jobs, killing herself to take care of Chance." He gestured with his Coke can. "She wouldn't let me see him."

"And you're still beating yourself up, taking the blame for his injury."

"Part of recovery. Own your mistakes. Make amends where you can. I'm going to make amends whether she likes it or not. Maybe not to her, but to him. I have to." He'd never be able to move forward until he did.

He'd loved Marisa, in his self-focused kind of way, and he'd cared about the young man who'd wanted to be like him. Still cared, if the truth was told, and lately he'd learned to be brutally honest with himself. Marisa was more than a mistake he'd made.

Emily coasted by in sneakers and rolled-up jeans, a red shirt the perfect foil to her black hair. His sister was a beauty. Levi was a lucky man, and the cowboy was smart enough to know it this time.

"When are those going to be ready?" Emily lifted her nose to sniff the air. "Everything else is on the tables, and I'm starving."

"I thought you were living on love these days." Ace tipped his Coke can toward Levi. The cowboy, baby now on his shoulder, made a beeline for his wife.

She grinned and snuggled her face into the baby's neck, sneaking a kiss to Levi during the exchange. "Love and steaks."

The newlyweds gazed at each other with such sappy adoration, Ace snickered. Had he ever felt that way about a woman?

Nate didn't seem the least bothered by the public display of affection. Probably because he'd been guilty of doing the same thing.

He interrupted the lovebirds. "Want yours rare, Emily?"

Emily managed to tear herself away from her husband to make a face. "Levi does. Not me. Medium is fine."

Nate stabbed a couple of rare steaks. The grill flamed up. "Those are ready for the red meat eaters." He handed the platter to her. "Ace went to see Marisa yesterday."

Steaks forgotten, his sister paused, expression sympathetic as her green eyes settled on Ace. "You okay?"

Ace heaved a heavy exhale. "I am. She's not. Neither is Chance. She's as skinny as a fence post. Lines and dark circles around her eyes. The whole exhausted look."

"With compliments like that, I'm surprised she didn't fall at your feet and plead with you to stay." Emily hefted the platter as Nate added two more steaks. "You should have invited her out today. We could fatten her up."

"She barely spoke to me and refused to do that for more than ten minutes. I doubt she'll let me feed her."

"What are you going to do?"

"I don't know. I've done what AA suggests, but it doesn't seem like enough. I want to do something to make her life better, easier. She needs help and is too proud to accept it." And he needed to prove to her that he was different now.

"Being overly proud is not uncommon for people who grew up in foster care. They have a distinct and understandable need to control their world."

This from a social worker who'd worked with plenty of foster kids. Like Daisy. "Any suggestions?"

One of the twins—Olivia, he thought—raced to Nate, waited until he bent for a hug, and then raced away, yelling something about daddy.

"Hey, Daddy." Whitney appeared, took the giant fork from Nate's hands, tugged the front of his shirt, and kissed him. Big brother got a sappy grin and wrapped her up like a burrito in his brawny arms.

Something twisted in Ace's gut that felt surprisingly like envy. He was thrilled for his brother's happiness, so why the sudden wish that *he* had a love and a family in his future?

Averting his gaze, he grabbed the fork and plated the rest of the steaks. When he looked up, Emily was watching him with the expression she always got when she was analyzing someone's behavior.

"What?"

"I'm sorry for the way Marisa responded to you. I can tell it hurts. We all see how hard you're trying, Ace. We see your progress." She touched his arm. "Want me to call her?"

He slammed the grill lid with a metallic clang that apparently served as a dinner bell for the rest of the crew. They immediately looked his way and then started toward the tables laden with food.

"I got this. It's my problem to fix."

About that time, Nate and Whitney came up for air.

Nate's grin was so big, his mouth was about to split. He noticed the steaks piled high on the platter in Emily's hands. "Sweet deal. Let's eat."

Nate looped an arm around his bride, hollered to the twins, and left the grill to Ace. Ace turned the appropriate knobs, then fell in step with his sister. As they reached the main table, his cell phone mooed. He loved that ring tone. Cows mooing sounded like money to him.

Stepping away from his sister and the noisy party, Ace answered the call and talked for a couple of minutes before hanging up.

"Nate. Can I talk to you for a second?" He punched a thumb over his shoulder.

Nate, his plate already piled with corn on the cob, steak and salad handed the dish to Whitney and came alongside Ace. "What's up?"

"A guy from AA. He got some bad news today, and he's wanting a drink." *Needing* a drink. Ace knew about that, too.

His salt-of-the-earth brother, jovial a minute ago, grew serious. "What can I do to help?"

Such was Nate. Always ready to lend a hand. Without him, Ace would never have gotten through the early days of sobriety. "I hate to miss the adoption celebration, but do you mind if I leave? I agreed to be this guy's sponsor, a new gig for me, and I promised to be there."

"Go. We'll save you a steak."

"Thanks." He patted his jeans' pocket for his truck keys, and, finding them, walked toward the parking area.

"Oh, and Ace?" Nate called behind him.

Ace spun on his boot heels. "Yeah?"

"I'm proud of you."

Warmth and love swelled in Ace's chest. Too moved to speak lest he make a fool of himself and choke up, he thumbed his Resistol, nodded once, and loped to his truck.

CARLA'S COUNTRY CAFÉ ON APPLEWOOD STREET in Clay City smelled good but nowhere near as good as his backyard. Ace ordered a basket of fries anyway. He was hungry, and having something to snack on helped keep his mind, and that of his AA pal, off the booze.

He probably shouldn't have chosen Carla's as the meeting place, but he'd always liked the laid back, homey atmosphere, and being here reminded him of the good times with Marisa. With Chance, too. Hanging out, having burgers, plotting the next adventure. The last part maybe wasn't so good, but the memories were.

"Want some tea or a Coke?" he said to the man sitting across from him at the square table for four. He didn't dare leave the question as open-ended as, "Want a drink?" The answer would most certainly be, yes, a fifth of vodka.

Dressed in a well-pressed, blue shirt and creased khakis, the blond, clean-cut man looked like a guy you'd sit by at church.

"I ordered before you got here. Thanks for meeting me." The man's hands shook as he fiddled with a classy watch on his wrist. The owner of a printing business, Don wasn't a jobless skid-row bum. He was a businessman, a functional alcoholic who'd thought he could handle the liquor. Who, like Ace, had long refused to believe he could be addicted. Also like Ace, he had the money to indulge in most anything he wanted, a dangerous thing for an alcoholic.

"So what's going on?" Ace asked. "You sounded pretty upset on the phone."

"My wife is going through with the divorce. I got the papers today." Don's eyes glistened suspiciously. He was forty-something with two young teenagers, and his wife had had her fill of his drinking, the weekends alone, the public embarrassment and subsequent fights.

"She doesn't believe you've changed."

"That's the problem." Don emitted a shaky breath. "I don't know if I have. I don't even know if I can."

Ace had felt the same way more than once. "You can, Don. You will. One day at a time, remember? Hang in there."

"I'm trying, but Joanie has no reason to believe that. I've made plenty of promises before." He leaned forward, hands squeezed together on the tabletop. "Without her, I have no reason to keep going."

"Yes, you do. Those boys will always be your sons. They need a sober father. The fact that you called me says a lot. You're fighting the good fight, and you'll win."

"Yeah, yeah." Don rotated his watch again. Sweat beaded on his forehead. He was fighting hard. "I guess I am."

The food arrived, a fragrant basket of crispy fries for Ace, chicken fried steak and gravy for Don. The steak reminded Ace of what he was missing back at the Triple C, but he kept that to himself. Getting food into an alcoholic helped keep him straight.

"I'll buy you a steak if you want it," Don said. "It's the least I can do."

"I'm good, but thanks."

"I might as well eat here. All I have at home is an empty fridge, and with Joanie gone, dinners don't happen." Face crumbling, he laid the fork on the edge of his plate. "What am I going to without her, Ace? She's my everything. She and the boys."

Ace had no answers, but he could listen and encourage, and that's what he did. When Don returned the favor, asking how Ace was doing, he told him about the run-in with Marisa.

Two drunks sharing sob stories. Weren't they awesome?

Regardless of Ace's sarcasm, meetings like this with his own sponsor had kept him sober plenty of times. Fortunately, he hadn't needed to make one of those calls in months.

When the food was gone, they ordered coffee and dawdled, talking some more. Ace listened and encouraged, repeating every platitude he'd learned in AA. Some-how, hokey as they sounded, they worked.

Finally, Don clinked his empty cup into a saucer and glanced at his watch. "It's getting late. I should let you go home."

"I'm here as long as you need."

The waitress appeared, coffee pot ready. Ace placed his hand over the top of his cup and shook his head. He was wired as it was. Some chamomile tea would sure hit the spot.

"Check please," he told the waitress. "One ticket."

"No, no, I've got it." Don fumbled for his wallet. "I'm the one who called you."

Ace captured the ticket from the waitress's hand. "You can get the next one. Just promise you'll call if the urge hits."

Don knew what urge he meant. The urge to drink, to numb the heartache of losing his family. "That's a promise I'll keep."

"Good. I'm praying for you, buddy. Hang in there."

Don rose from the table and pushed in his chair. "Does it ever get easier?"

Ace dropped a few bills on the table and followed him up. "If you mean will you ever stop wanting a drink, I don't know, but I can tell you this. After a while, the edge disappears and the air smells cleaner, the sky is bluer, and you start living again. Really living."

"Without my family?"

Tough call, and Ace wasn't one to blow smoke. "Don't give up hope. She loved you once. Maybe she will again when she sees you've changed this time."

The words reverberated in Ace's ears. Marisa had loved him once. And he desperately wanted her to believe he'd changed. Not that he had any hope of rekindling their love affair, but his need to make amends gnawed like a giant Norway rat.

Don, who had calmed considerably in the two hours in the café, smiled for the first time. "I've got a lot to prove, but I'm up for it. Thanks, Ace. Thanks a lot."

"Anytime."

Don turned and walked out the door, holding it open while a beautiful brunette strolled into the cafe. Her gaze fell on Ace, and a slow, knowing smile curved sensuous lips as she looked him up and down.

"Well, hello, my Ace of diamonds. Long time no see."

Ace's stomach took a tumble. Meeting old drinking friends was inevitable, but this one was a true temptation. "Kristen."

She sauntered up to him in tight jeans and pink boots, the top three buttons on her blouse undone. Her perfume, an expensive brand he liked, floated around her, pulled him in.

"I've been thinking about you. Where did you disappear to?"

"Working cows and keeping my head down."

She laughed. "Now, why don't I believe that?"

"It's true." He held up both palms.

"You know what they say. All work and no play means it's time for you to have some fun. Want to take me out to the club tonight? Call some friends." She ran a finger up the center of his chest and tapped his chin. "Have a little reunion party?"

The temptation roared in like a wildfire. He'd once enjoyed Kristen's crazy, adventurous side. The woman knew how to party.

He repeated the words he'd said to Marisa. "I don't do that anymore."

Her hand, busy roaming his biceps, paused. "You're joking."

Using every bit of willpower he didn't know he had, Ace removed Kristen's hand from his body and let it drop. "Dead serious."

She took one step back to stare up at his face. "I think you are."

"I am."

She studied him for another second or two while he prayed inwardly and battled the desire to follow her out the door.

Finally, Kristen tossed her gorgeous brown hair and laughed. "Do me one little favor?"

"What would that be?"

She tapped his cheek and winked. "Call me when you get over it."

Then, she laughed again, whirled on her pretty pink boots and left him standing in a cold sweat.

MARISA STEPPED around the corner of the building and watched the long, lean cowboy exit Carla's Country Café. She didn't want him to see her, especially after what she'd observed. She didn't want another confrontation with Ace Caldwell now or ever. He did unhealthy things to her head, and she was still recovering from the insanity of the last time.

But she had to admit, the cowboy looked good in his boots and jeans with the silver, custom-made Triple C belt buckle his daddy had given him for his sixteenth birthday. Funny, the things she remembered about him—little details that would jump out once in a while and startle her with their intensity.

Like this café. What were the chances that he'd be here on the first night she'd ventured back to their old haunt? Not that she would have come without incentive, but Chance, who showed little interest in anything, had expressed a yearning for Carla's hand-pattied bacon cheeseburger with salsa, grilled onions and jalapeño peppers.

So here she was like some kind of voyeur, staring in the window at Ace talking to a gorgeous brunette. Kristen Fairchild, a rich daddy's darling in a pink Jeep that Marisa remembered from high school. A woman who made Marisa's scrubs and ponytail seem faded and dull by comparison.

Kristen wouldn't remember her, not by a long shot. They'd run in vastly different circles. She'd seen the way the woman had come on to Ace, the way she'd put her hands on him as if they knew each other better than an unmarried couple should. Kristen liked men, and they liked her right back.

For a moment before she'd hustled away from the window to hide, Marisa wondered if Ace was one of Kristen's men. But he hadn't returned Kristen's flirty looks or smiles. He'd stepped away from her invasive touch, and the woman had stormed out, her expression annoyed as she hopped into her Jeep and roared away.

Maybe Ace was cleaning up his act.

But she wasn't willing to bet Chance's health on it. Or her heart.

CHAPTER 4

*G*etting into the Sunset Manor Care Center wasn't nearly as complicated as Ace had expected. A couple of phone calls, a donation to the right department, and he sailed right through the front door with the security code in hand.

The odor hit him first. Nothing like a hospital, the care center slapped him with a mix of cooked foods, none of which smelled anything like Connie's kitchen at the Triple C, and the more disturbing body smells. How did anyone eat in here?

Slowly, he looked around at the lobby area where several wheelchair-parked elderly and infirm talked or stared into space. One man slept, his head at a painful angle against his chest.

An overwhelming sense of despair washed over Ace. Chance lived here. The strong, athletic young man was doomed to live his life here. Because of Ace Caldwell.

Rubbing a hand over his face, Ace tried to shake off

41

the melancholy. This care center was no different than hundreds of others. Not bad. Not great. But it served a purpose. And the fact that Marisa worked here told him that Chance and every other resident would get the best care possible in a residential facility. Which only made Ace feel worse. How could this kind of life be ideal for anyone?

A nurse's aide passed by wheeling a sprightly man with a Bible in his lap. He caught Ace's stare and winked. "Off to see my girlfriends in the rec room."

His attitude lifted the corners of Ace's lips. He tapped his forehead in a salute. "Enjoy."

As the man was wheeled away, Ace noticed his feet. He had none.

Lights over the doorways pinged, and more nurses hurried inside the rooms. They were trying. But how did anyone beat back the infirmities of age?

And why had he never been inside a nursing home before? The thought shamed him. He'd spent so much time in selfish pursuits that he hadn't noticed the hardships of others.

Another item for his list.

Was this God's way of opening his eyes?

After a stop at the nurse's station, where he was warned that Chance was "in a mood" today and refused to do anything, Ace found his way down a tiled hall, past opened doors that should have been closed, and entered room sixteen.

Fortunately, Marisa was not yet on duty for her evening shift, another piece of information he'd gotten from the facility's administrator. He also knew she worked at a daycare before coming here.

Chance's room was identical to the others Ace had seen as he'd come down the hall—a nightstand, a rolling dinner tray, a chair, a TV, a bed, and a wheelchair. Someone— Marisa, he supposed—had hung some colorful framed pictures on the wall. A scripture stencil above the bed and a bouquet of blue plastic flowers on the nightstand rounded out the décor. Not much, but something to dispel the gloom.

Chance lay in the bed staring up at the ceiling. When he saw Ace, he turned away. It wasn't an easy task. First, he rotated his upper body, and then his hands disappeared beneath the sheet to drag his legs until his back was to the door. The action seared into Ace.

Now that he was here, he wasn't sure what to do. He stood awkwardly, arms dangling at his sides. He shifted his weight, his boots scraping the tile floor.

"Look, Chance. I know you don't want me around. I get that. You probably despise the thought of me. I get that, too, and I deserve it."

His former friend didn't respond.

"An apology seems pretty lame at this point, but that's all I've got. If I could go back, erase that night, I would. If I could change places with you, I would. Nobody wants to be where you are, but I'd do it."

His chest started to ache. Regret was a hot iron pressing inside, burning and branding him.

"Do you need anything I can get for you? Is there anything I can do? Let me somehow make this up to you." As soon as the words escaped, he wanted them back. He dropped his head back, stared at the ceiling. "That was stupid. Nothing can ever make up for what you've lost. I'm sorry. God knows I mean that."

He waited, praying for a response and getting none.

He wasn't sure what he'd expected—rage maybe—but not this cold silence.

He'd searched for Marisa and Chance because of his need for absolution, but a light had dawned in his sober brain as he'd traversed the halls of Chance's new dwelling. God had sent him to this place for a reason beyond his own selfish needs. This wasn't about him. It was about finding a way to help Chance.

MARISA THOUGHT the top of her head would explode. She stood facing the nurse's desk, trembling with fury.

"I left explicit instructions that no one was to go into that room without my permission!"

Two residents turned to stare and three nurses came out of nearby rooms. Aware she was on the verge of yelling, Marisa modulated her voice. She swallowed, tried to calm down. And failed.

"Who let him in there?"

Sandy, the rotund nurse on duty, lifted both hands in surrender. "I don't know. Wasn't me."

"Never mind. I'll take care of this." Spinning on her tennis shoes, Marisa stormed down the hallway to Chance's room and marched inside, ready to blast the sorry excuse for a cowboy and protect her baby brother.

Ace stood close to the bed, hat dangling at his side. He pivoted, boots scraping, when she entered. One look at his expression, and Marisa's anger dissipated. He appeared wounded, lost, defeated.

When had Ace Caldwell ever been defeated?

She glanced toward her brother. He lay with his back to them, a common ploy he used when he didn't want to talk, didn't want company. She'd seen that move many times.

"I warned you not to come here again."

Green eyes that had once haunted her dreams fell shut. After a second, he moved closer to the bed and bowed his head.

Was he praying?

A minute later, he drew a deep breath and left the room. No argument. No conversation. He just walked out the door.

Remorse, and maybe pity, shuddered through Marisa. Before she could think better of the action, she followed Ace down the hall and caught up with him.

"Ace."

He stopped, broad shoulders slumped. "Go ahead and say I told you so or ban me again, but you won't stop me."

She stepped around in front of him. "Why? Why can't you leave us in peace?"

"You call that peace?" He gestured toward Chance's room. "Now that I've seen him, there's no way I can leave him like this."

Marisa bristled. "You think I'm not trying?"

"I think you're *killing* yourself trying." His voice was soft and kind, and the concern nearly broke her.

Marisa rubbed at the ever-present tension in her neck.

"And *he* won't try at all. He's depressed and bitter and angry."

"Isn't that normal? Wouldn't you be?"

"The doctors say he should have snapped out of it by now. We've had counselors and pastors, even medication. He refuses to take the drugs, and he won't talk to anyone. He ignores the doctors the same way he ignored you."

She didn't say the rest. She'd run out of money to pay counselors and doctors. Since they'd long ago stopped helping Chance, they were one expense she could avoid. Disability paid for his room but did not pay for the rehab extras he needed, and any insurance money he'd received was long gone on medical bills.

"What about his old friends and his students? Would he talk to them?"

"He doesn't want them to see him like this."

"There has to be something we can do."

"If there is, I'm at a loss."

"Will you let me try?"

"I don't understand why you'd want to."

"I owe him."

She agreed, but his quiet sincerity also affected her, and his gentle concern for Chance seemed real.

She didn't want to be soft around him. Ace was dangerous. To her. To Chance. But he wasn't drinking, and a sober Ace had always gotten through her defenses.

"I have to get to work," she said.

"Your shift doesn't start until three."

She shouldn't have been surprised that he knew her hours. After all, he'd hired a private investigator. "I'm covering a few hours for another nursing assistant."

"I see." He fiddled with his hat, eyes on the gray felt. "Meet me for coffee when you get off at eleven."

"Coffee?" She scoffed. "What about a beer? Or a couple of tequila shots?"

She was feeling mean and angry, but her words had an odd effect.

He glanced up, his gaze as cool as green glass. "Coffee's fine."

His reaction puzzled her. No jaunty grin or joke. Just that long, solemn stare.

"I can't." Wouldn't.

"Carla's. Eleven o'clock."

"Still have trouble with the no word, don't you, cowboy?"

"This is too important. *Chance* is too important."

He had her there. Chance was the single most important person in her life, and he would be from now on.

"I don't know what you can do that a dozen doctors haven't tried." The mighty Caldwells thought they could do anything.

"I don't either, but we can't give up, Marisa. He's only twenty-five years old."

He had her there.

"I can't meet you tonight." After the extra hours today, she'd be a dead woman walking by eleven. Not that she would share that fact with him.

"Tomorrow then. Meet me for lunch."

A battle ensued in Marisa's head. Ace only wanted a balm for his guilt. But her little brother needed all the encouragement he could get. Ace was the last man on earth she should be around, and she certainly didn't want his blood money. But maybe if she talked to him he would go away for good.

"All right, then. Tomorrow at noon at Carla's."

Before she could do anything else stupid, she whipped around and headed for the break room to clock in. He might think he'd won, but she would never let down the wall that had taken her nearly two years to build.

SHE DIDN'T GET to Carla's Country Cafe until twelve thirty, and she hoped Ace would have given up by then. But as soon as she walked into the café, she saw him seated at a table next to the window, facing the door.

A wave of nostalgia swooshed over her. The two of them at that table, holding hands, smiling into each other's eyes as if there were no one else in the universe. Making plans that never happened.

She stiffened her spine and stuffed the memories. She would not be that foolish again.

The building was crowded, the square tables filled as they always were at noon, and the smell of freshly cooked food made her belly weep. Eating out was a rare treat. Very rare.

Ace stood as she approached the table, his southern boy manners as much a part of him as his green eyes. Those eyes had been the first thing she'd noticed all those years ago, and she noticed them now.

"Busy morning?"

She settled in the chair he'd pulled out. "Very."

"How long is your lunch break?"

"An hour."

"Not long enough." He smiled. Not the playboy grin of yesteryear but a genuine smile. "We'll have to do this again."

"I work two jobs. Time off is nearly impossible."

"And you pull doubles, work everyone else's sick days, fill in for any and every one who asks."

She shrugged, refusing to feel sorry for herself. "That's life in the real world."

The waitress arrived and slid a plastic menu in front of each of them. She looked like a college student, young, blond and tanned, with perfect teeth in a perfect smile. Marisa ignored the pinch of envy. Life was what it was. This was her path, and she'd walk it.

"I already know what I want." Marisa returned the menu with a polite smile.

"Me, too." And before she could brace for it, he caught her eye and ordered exactly what she had in mind. "Did I get it right?"

Grudgingly, she admitted, "Yes. Thanks. With sweet tea."

She didn't want him remembering her favorite foods or treating this like a date. It wasn't. It was a barely civil meeting that she'd only agreed to in hopes of soothing a conscience that shouldn't hate anyone but did. She had no hope that the cowboy could do anything for Chance that hadn't already been tried without success.

The young waitress scribbled the orders and hurried away, stopping at tables along the path to the kitchen. The cacophony of voices in the room was enough to cover any conversation. The problem was, now that she was here, she didn't know what to say.

Ace made her nervous. She wanted to be angry. He needed to go away and never return. She couldn't have another drunk in her life. She was too genetically prone to fall for them.

The young waitress returned with the cold drinks. Marisa reached for hers as if it were a lifeline.

Ace ignored his. "Tell me about him."

She gulped the iced tea, the cold sweetness pleasant. "What do you want to know?"

"Everything."

"He's paralyzed from the waist down. He'll never walk again, much less play ball or coach or dance at his own wedding."

Ace had the grace to wince. If she'd made him uncomfortable, she refused to be sorry. Chance's disability was his fault.

"I know that much. Tell me about rehab. About the last eighteen months."

So he'd counted down the months since the accident. Big deal. So had she. Minutes, hours, days of praying that God would make her brother whole again.

"There's a spinal cord rehabilitation hospital in Houston. We went there when he was stable enough to travel." She'd found a job and a tiny apartment nearby, alternating between work and the hospital. "It's a top-ten facility, so I had hopes..."

Hopes that never materialized.

"And when the money ran out, you brought him back home."

She rubbed her fingers up and down the moist tea glass. "My finances are none of your business, Ace."

Instead of the argument she'd expected, he said, "I'm glad you're home."

So was she. "The doctors thought being back in his home town, around the familiar, would elevate Chance's spirits."

"But it hasn't."

"If anything, his mood is worse here. It's as if he's given up."

"He's in a nursing home, Marisa, and he's a young man. It would be hard not to give up."

The remark infuriated her, but it defeated her too. "What choice do I have? I can't take care of him at home and hold a job, too. Sunset Manor was the best solution. At least there, I can be with him eight hours a day."

He tilted his head, expression wry. "Or more."

On days off from the daycare, whenever possible, she worked extra at the nursing home, and vice versa. It was the only way she could manage, another fact she didn't share with Ace.

Their food arrived, two identical plates of barbecue brisket with all the fixings and a basket of fragrant, buttery yeast rolls.

Her stomach reminded her of the meals she'd skipped yesterday. "I'd forgotten how amazing this smells."

"Tastes even better, but let's pray first."

Surprise jolted her, but Marisa bowed her head while he murmured a simple blessing. When he prayed for Chance and ended with, "Thank you, Father, for sobriety, and grant me the grace for one more day," Marisa opened her eyes to stare at him.

Was he for real? Or was this a sneaky way of getting

back on her good side? He'd pushed aside her faith during their dating days and had displayed none of his own. His family were Christians. And he'd been brought up to believe. But he hadn't.

After the amen, he reached for his fork and stabbed a bite of brisket.

Disconcerted, Marisa adjusted her napkin. "What was that all about?"

The fork paused at his mouth. She remembered those lips and didn't want to.

"What?"

"Sobriety?"

"I joined AA, got sober for good. It was about time."

She wasn't sure if she believed him. Remembering all the times he'd scoffed at the idea that he'd become a problem drinker, all the times he'd claimed he could quit any time he wanted to. He just hadn't wanted to.

"Your family must be delighted."

Something moved through his expression. "They've been supportive. But let's talk about Chance and you."

Only Chance. Not her. She wasn't letting him get that close. "What else is there to say? He's crippled and depressed and the future looks dismal."

"If things are that bad, what harm is there in my spending time with him?"

Because seeing you hurts too much. You make me remember how it felt to be loved and to love in return, to love and hate all in the same breath, and that's too dangerous. You're too dangerous.

"Not a good idea."

"I'm going to see him, Marisa, with your permission or without it."

"Then why ask me to meet you? Why bother with this pretend concern and sobriety?"

"I'm not pretending." He put his fork across the edge of his plate. "I want us to work together. I hoped the two of us together could come up with ideas to motivate Chance and get him dreaming again."

Guilt. It had to be his guilt. But he was wearing her down. He'd always been able to do that. And she was sucker enough to fall for it.

This time, he was petitioning for Chance.

"I'm afraid I'm all out of ideas."

"That's because you're tired. You've carried this for nearly two years. Let me carry it now."

He was such a smooth talker. The man should be a politician.

"I won't object if you visit him sometimes. But try not to upset him, and don't expect me to be around. I'm not interested in rekindling the very ugly past."

He winced and lowered his eyes. Her words had hit their mark.

As she was strangling on the needed apology, a man walked up to the table.

"Ace. I thought that was you. How's it going?"

"Hanging in there. You?"

"The same."

The two men talked for a few minutes, and she noticed that Ace hadn't bothered to introduce her. He was usually more polite than that, and she started to wonder. Was the man someone he didn't want her know? One of his drinking buddies, perhaps?

After the man left, Ace deftly moved the conversation to the ranch, the recent weddings of his brother and sister, and the three new children that had been added to his family.

She listened with half-hearted interest, her mind churning with suspicion. Had he really turned over a new leaf?

As she finished her meal, the facts settled with the barbecue. Her entire life, and Chance's, had been damaged by alcoholics. They'd both endured too much loss, grief and disaster to ever take another chance.

CHAPTER 5

For the ninth evening in a row, Ace slipped into Chance's room and began to talk. His family at the ranch understood his need to be at Sunset Manor and gave him the grace to miss dinner, though Connie fretted that he'd turn to skin and bones. He worked the ranch all day, but as soon as the chores were finished, he headed for Clay City. The paperwork and books could wait until he returned. Late nights hadn't affected him during the drinking days. They sure wouldn't now that he didn't wake with a pounding hangover.

Some days when he arrived at the center, Chance was in his wheelchair. On bad days, he remained in bed. No matter his location, he'd turned his back every time Ace entered the room.

Undeterred, Ace continued to talk about anything and everything. He filled the younger man in on ranch activities, new colts and calves, Connie's flower beds, Gilbert's battle with his blood sugar, the nieces, nephew, brothers and sister. Yesterday, he'd shared about AA, something he hadn't planned to do, but the kid deserved to know that the tragedy had affected him enough to take action.

When he ran out of words, he sat in silence or turned on the TV and offered commentary on the programming, most of it snarky and intended to make Chance laugh. So far, he was batting zero.

His throat was wearing out from all the one-sided conversation and he must have sucked on a thousand cinnamon disks. If he was frustrated by the lack of response, he couldn't imagine what Marisa had endured over the last year and a half.

Ace ended each visit by reading the Bible and saying a prayer. He wasn't too good at praying yet, but God didn't care about fancy. Anyway, Ace hoped He didn't.

Though Marisa had vowed never to step inside the room when he was there, she couldn't stay away. Not because she wanted to be friendly, but because she was a control freak making sure he did nothing to harm her brother. Making sure Chance was cool enough or warm enough and that his space was tidy, his sheets straight, his feet braced at the appropriate angle.

It killed him the way she wore herself out trying to fix the unfixable.

Maybe he was doing the same thing.

Every time she walked into the room, "I told you so" seemed to pour from her eyes. Not sympathy. Resignation.

But he wouldn't give up. He had Connie and the whole family praying, and when Connie prayed, God listened.

The little Mexican woman could pray the house down. He credited her prayers with the fact that God had kept him alive throughout his wild escapades.

"Hey, bud, I brought my cards." He tapped the new deck on the bedside table and shuffled it with a loud *prrrrr*. "What'll it be? Texas Hold'em? Seven Card Stud? Pick your poison."

When Chance didn't reply, Ace began to deal. "Texas Hold'em, you say? Better have plenty of toothpicks, because you are in the presence of a master."

As if Chance was participating, Ace rattled all the nonsense men say to each other on a challenge. Whether shooting baskets or casting a rod and reel, he and Chance had thrived on good-spirited competition. Tonight, however, his friend ignored his challenge. So, Ace played for them both.

After a couple of rounds, Marisa appeared at the door, glanced at the two hands of cards spread on the table and stepped inside. "Who's winning?"

"He is," Ace said. "But he's cheating."

For an instant, he thought he heard a grunt from the bed. Marisa heard it too and stepped closer to her brother. "Chance? You want to play for real?"

Her brother didn't budge. Marisa turned back to the table, lifted Chance's hole cards and pushed two toothpicks toward the middle. "And raise you two more."

"It's getting serious now." Ace gnawed at his lip as if this were a life-or-death match. To his pleasure, Marisa snickered. He wouldn't mind if she warmed up a little more often. Not that he blamed her for loathing the very air he breathed, but the constant cold shoulder was giving him pneumonia.

He dealt the remaining cards, and to his happy surprise, Marisa beat the socks off him. Twice.

He pretended despair. "She's killing me, Chance. Kicking my tail. At this rate, she'll own every toothpick in Oklahoma. I'll have to sell the ranch."

"Better believe it, cowboy. Slick-fingered Marisa is my name. Toothpicks are my game."

They'd kept up the banter all through the game, hoping for a response from Chance, both of them especially attuned to the silent man on the bed. This was the Marisa he'd known and loved. Competitive, fun-loving, smart. Hardship had stolen her smile. But her occasional laugh and the sparkle in her eyes told him the woman he remembered was still in there.

Her pager buzzed, and she tossed her cards on the table. "You're on your own, Chance. Duty calls. If I were you, I'd keep an eye on Ace's left shirt sleeve."

She patted her brother's back, kissed his ear and started toward the door.

"Hey." Ace stopped her. He wanted her to stay.

She glanced back over one shoulder, smirking. "Ready to admit I'm the best at poker? Go ahead. I'm listening."

She looked so tired, but for once, she was smiling at him. Ace shuffled the cards, feeling a little tug behind his ribcage. "I wanted to say thanks."

Her jaunty expression faltered. "I do this for Chance. No thanks wanted."

Following that cold shot to the lungs, she left him alone.

MARISA WAS SURROUNDED. In a good way.

She sat Indian-style on the brightly colored alphabet rug inside Kids' Care Playschool, reading *Llama, Llama Red Pajama* to her charges. This morning she was so tired, sitting for a few minutes felt great.

Tabitha, a freckled darling with big blue eyes, hopped to her feet and began a familiar dance. "Potty."

Marisa hopped up, too, and swept the child under one arm like a football player making a run for the goal line. Teaching the two-and three-year-old class meant potty training, which meant staying on her toes.

When she and Tabitha returned, her co-worker, Clare, was finishing up the much-loved story.

As soon as the book closed, the children scattered, their attention span at its limit.

With a tender smile, Marissa watched the children scramble around the brightly colored, kid-friendly room. She loved working here among the little ones. At nearly thirty-three and with Chance to care for, Marissa had faced the fact that she might never have kids of her own, but these babies filled her need to mother and gave her more to think about than her problems.

Kids' Care was, indeed, the perfect job to coordinate with her shifts at Sunset Manor. Located in a residential neighborhood of Clay City a few blocks off Main Street, the older home had been converted into a daycare some years ago.

She turned her attention to her coworker. "Thanks, Clare."

The other woman slid the completed board book onto the shelf. It wouldn't stay there long. The kids would have it and others spread over the rug when the notion struck. Picking up was an endless task.

"You look tired today." Clare stepped closer, eyebrows drawn together. "You look tired every day, but today more than usual. Is everything okay with Chance?"

Though she'd worked at Kids' Care only three months, Marisa had become friendly with Clare Farley, a twenty-something redhead who could talk the bark off a tree. Though Marisa hadn't shared everything, Clare knew about her brother's paraplegia.

"Chance is okay." A big fat lie. Her brother would never be okay. "I didn't sleep well." Again. "That's all."

Thank you, Ace Caldwell, for another restless night. She didn't know why the man didn't give up and leave them alone, but he kept hanging around like a bad cough. Chance ignored him, and she tried her best to freeze him out. The trouble was, she couldn't. His persistence touched her a little bit. And he brought back memories, some good and some bad, but the good ones kept sneaking in. Especially after lunch at Carla's Country Café.

Ace Caldwell had everything a man could want. Money, looks, personality, and a big, loving family. He'd made his apologies, for whatever good they were. Why did he bother with her and Chance?

She still wasn't sure she bought his story about AA and making amends. The Ace she'd known would rather choke than admit he was at fault or that he needed help.

"I don't know how you juggle two jobs." Clare bent to

wipe Bryce's drippy nose with a tissue. The two-year-old jerked his head to one side. Clare caught him and tried again, succeeding this time. "With Ted and the babies, I can barely handle one. I'm lucky to be able to bring Cassidy and Katie with me to work."

"The perks of working in a daycare." A perk Marisa would never get to enjoy.

"What you need is a break and some fun."

A tiny blonde cutie grabbed Clare's legs in a hug. Clare gave the little back a pat and kept right on talking. "Ted and I are having a few people over Saturday to grill brats and hang out. Would you like to come?"

Marisa was already shaking her head. "I wish I could."

"Working, I guess." Clare lifted her eyebrows. "Or is there a mysterious man in the picture you haven't told me about?"

The picture of a tall, rangy cowboy flashed through Marisa's head. She forced a laugh. "One could only wish. My knight in shining armor is probably rusted by now."

Clare laughed, then sobered. "I can introduce you to some guys. Ted has a couple of single friends."

"All younger than me, I'm sure."

"You're not that old."

She felt a hundred most days. "Getting there fast. But thank you for the invitation. I have work at Sunset Manor."

Church was about the only activity she had time for, and she couldn't always attend. The idea of going out and enjoying herself with friends was almost foreign. But a longing rose to do exactly that.

"What about Bryce's dad, Brent Murray? He's pretty cute and around your age."

She'd noticed the big, quiet man who dropped his son off every morning at seven. He had a nice smile and clearly loved his baby boy. "Wouldn't Bryce's mom object to that?"

"Oh, I keep forgetting you don't know everyone the way I do. Brent's divorced and has custody of Bryce. His wife left right after Bryce was born."

"Wow, that's sad."

"Mmm-hmm. Real sad. You should cheer him up."

Marisa made a rude noise. "What are you, the daycare matchmaker?"

"Hey! I like that idea. I'll get right on it. A couple of the other teachers are single, and I'm sure we have other single dads."

Marisa waved a hand in the air, effectively erasing the offer. "Leave me out. No time." And no heart for romance. She was still picking up the pieces from the last time.

"Okay, okay, but let me know when you're ready. I'll hook you up." Clare glanced at the big clock on the wall. "Oops. We gotta move. It's outside time. I'll fill sippy cups if you'll get the stroller."

Shaking her head at Clare's youthful enthusiasm, Marisa commandeered the kid cart, a six-seat stroller, and began loading children. Clare took the hands of the remaining two and led them outside onto the playground.

Big trees shaded the small fenced area of climbing toys, crawl tubes, and a little play house with a tot-sized table. Marisa grabbed a bottle of water from the cart and joined Clare at the picnic table to watch the little ones play. The early June sun played hide and seek with the tree limbs, and a breeze rustled the leaves.

"We have several absent today." Marisa gazed around the playground. "I wonder if there's a virus going around."

Clare shook her head, caught a lock of blowing hair, and hooked it behind one ear. "Didn't you hear about the new day care over by the elementary school?"

"I heard Janey say something about it. Why?" A sliver of worry teased the back of her neck. "Are we losing people?"

Without kids, she had no job.

Clare grimaced. "The two Baker children and one of the infants in the baby room."

"That's not good."

"We may lose more. Sherry Jackson mentioned something about moving her three kids."

"Why? Are we doing something wrong?" The thought terrified her. Without any training other than her nurse aide certification, where else would she find an extra job so perfectly suited to her needs and interests? She didn't mind the work at Sunset Manor, but she loved this one. Once upon a lost dream, she'd hoped for college and a teaching degree. That would never happen now.

"The new place is offering a discount for the first six months, and they're open seven days a week." Clare shot up from her seat, separated a pair of toddlers arguing over a plastic truck, and returned to the table. "Day care is expensive, especially when you have several kids, and if the new place is cheaper and available more, we could be in trouble."

Kids' Care was closed on weekends, a problem for some working families.

"Does Janey know?" Janey was their boss and owner of Kids' Care.

"She knows. And she's worried."

"Couldn't she offer a discount, too?"

"If she does, she'll have to cut back in other areas."

Other areas. As in employees.

If enough children moved to the new daycare center, Marisa's job could be in jeopardy.

One of the little ones stumbled and fell. Marisa rose and started toward him as he began to cry. She wanted to cry, too.

What if she lost this job? How would she pay for Chance's care and still whittle down the mountain of medical bills that never stopped appearing in her mailbox?

As she crouched on the grass to dust the little boy's hands and dry his tears, one thought kept echoing in her head.

Last one hired, first one fired. And hers was the last head on the chopping block.

FOR THE NEXT THREE WEEKS, Marisa held her breath as a few more parents moved their children to the new child care facility. Though she and Clare remarked on the losses, nothing was said about cutting staff. Finally, she began to relax again. She had enough to worry about with Chance and the lean cowboy who refused to go away.

She'd grown accustomed to seeing Ace in the care

center. The trouble was, she couldn't seem to keep her distance and was thankful that her job kept her from hanging out too long in one spot.

Ace had made not one bit of progress with her brother, but still he came. Seeing him there and listening outside the door to his endless chatter got to her, touched her. He'd always had the ability to break down her walls, and she had to keep reminding herself of what he'd done the last time she'd let him in. Ace's magnetism was like a black hole, mysterious and dangerous, with no way to get out.

Not once had he shown up smelling of alcohol, but she figured it was only a matter of time. In the past, he could go days without a drink, but then he'd binge. Like he had on Chance's birthday.

He couldn't hide the real Ace forever. This time, she'd be ready.

Peeking into her brother's room, she saw the back of Chance's dark head and the sheet he'd tugged up to his ears. Ace sat in the only chair, long legs stretched out in front, reading from the Bible.

Marisa wasn't sure if she appreciated the effort or hated it. This side of Ace gave her problems, and she didn't want to think of him as a good guy. Smoke and mirrors, she'd decided, a façade to assuage his guilt.

Hurrying away before he saw her and coerced her inside the room, she helped her co-workers ready the residents for sleep and prepare for the oncoming night shift.

Two nurses had developed a mad crush on the long-legged cowboy, and the other staff considered him a hottie and poked their heads into Chance's room every time they went past. The male workers teased her about having a new man. And Sandy, the LPN, had started wearing makeup again, something she hadn't done since her divorce. The hoopla over Ace was becoming ridiculous.

They didn't know what she did.

She clicked off the light in her final room and pulled the door closed. Mrs. Reynolds was a sweetheart, and except for Chance, Marisa saved her room for last so they could pray together.

Lately, her prayers felt flat, as if the pipeline between her and God were stopped up with debris. But she was too busy and tired from caring for her brother to figure out the problem.

Tonight had been particularly hectic, and her legs ached. She wanted nothing more than a hot bath and a cozy bed.

She paused outside Chance's room, listening for Ace's quiet baritone. When she heard nothing, she went in. Ace was still in the chair, the Bible open on his lap.

"Time to go home, Ace. Chance needs his rest."

He quirked an eyebrow, and Marisa read the expression as clearly as if he'd spoken. *Chance rests all the time. Look where that's got him.*

She thought the same thing, but she wouldn't tell Ace.

He closed the book and stood, his tall body filling up the space. Marisa passed in front of him, more aware of his closeness than she wanted to be, and went around to the opposite side of the bed to face her brother.

"My shift is over, Chance. Do you want me to bring you anything tomorrow?"

Her brother's navy eyes opened. "No."

She glanced up to see the pain on Ace's face. Chance had spoken to her but not to him. She didn't want to feel sorry for the cowboy, but the tug was there.

"I love you."

"You, too." The barely audible words ended on an exhausted sigh.

She kissed his cheek and, with a heart full of sorrow for her once vibrant young brother, exited the room. She didn't dare glance back at Ace.

After clocking out, she grabbed her purse from the locker, called a soft good-night to her coworkers, and headed to her car. The night air had cooled, and the smell of rain hung on the barely breeze. Wispy clouds scudded across the moon. April was fickle, hot one day, cool the next, with plenty of rain and the occasional storm tossed in to keep things interesting.

She sucked in the clean, fresh air and willed her shoulders to relax as she unlocked her car and slid inside.

Clay City was a safe town. She'd never been threatened, but the shadowy parking lot spooked her at night. Usually, she waited for another staff member to walk her out, but tonight she'd been in a hurry to avoid Ace.

She clicked her locks and then cranked the engine. The starter churned and churned, but the motor refused to kick in.

She tried again. Same result.

"Please, please, God, not now." She turned the key again. Nothing.

With a frustrated groan, Marisa dropped her head back against the headrest. What now? No mechanic was available at eleven o'clock at night, and even if one walked up to her car right this minute, she couldn't afford car repairs.

She was too tired for this.

Frustrated, she glanced around the parking lot but knew full well that not one of her coworkers could help. Maybe one of them would drive her home.

That wouldn't work. She had to be at the daycare by six. How could she get there if her car was here?

Ace. He hadn't left yet. His truck was still parked in the lot.

No way. She would not ask him.

Her eyes strayed to the big black pickup. Out of the shadows, Ace appeared, and the truck lights flashed as he unlocked with his key fob. Before he got inside, he peered in her direction. Why had he done that?

Then he climbed inside his vehicle and backed out.

There went her best hope, thanks to her stubborn pride.

But he didn't leave. To her surprise and relief, he pulled the truck behind her car and got out. She opened her door.

"Trouble?" He moved into her space, leaning down as if he could see the problem in the front seat.

"It won't start."

"Try it again."

With an aggravated sigh, she did. The result was the same. Nothing.

Ace hitched a thumb toward his truck. "Get in. I'll take you home."

Marisa gripped the steering wheel as if he'd threatened to drag her out and kidnap her. Being alone with Ace was not a good idea.

"Can't. I have to have my car. I work in the morning at six."

"I'll come back after I drop you off and see if I can discover the problem. Get in the truck. You need sleep. You look half dead."

If she'd had the energy, she would have argued more, but she didn't, because he was right. She *was* half dead.

She climbed into his truck, the leather soft and fragrant. For a working rancher, he kept a very clean vehicle. "What if you can't figure out the problem?"

Ace shifted the gears and drove onto the street, the big engine purring like a massive kitten while Marisa's car was as silent as road kill. "I'm pretty handy. Let me worry about your car."

"I can't. Surely, you understand that."

"I do understand. I just don't like it." He shot her a quick glance, huffed noisily. "Can't you see I'm trying?"

"All the trying in the world won't bring Chance's legs back to life." It was that. It was always that.

In the dash lights, she saw his eyes close briefly. She'd been intentionally cruel, needing to hurt him, needing a reason to remember what he'd done, but this time, she felt no victory, only shame.

Why should she be the one who felt guilty? He was at fault.

The argument didn't seem as strong as it once had.

The rest of the ride was silent until Ace slowed, clicked on his turn signal, and pulled the truck into her driveway.

She should say something nice. After all, he'd driven her home, but words wouldn't come. He confused her, reminding her of both the good and the bad and stirring old feelings like embers in a campfire. She couldn't allow those embers to burst into flame.

Shifting into park, his handsome face aglow in the dash lights, Ace swiveled his upper body. His eyes settled on her, somber. "Good night, Marisa. Get some sleep."

"My key fob. You'll need it."

Ace extended a hand. Their fingers brushed in the transfer. An unwanted tingle shimmied up Marisa's arm. She dropped the key in his palms and jerked away to shove a shoulder against the heavy door. Quickly, she slid to the ground before he could do the southern boy thing and walk her to the porch. She couldn't take that. Not tonight when she was feeling vulnerable and guilty. Not when she was remembering the sweet things about Ace Caldwell.

"Thank you."

The dome light illuminated him. He looked tired too, but fatigue didn't dim his good looks or his cowboy masculinity. "No problem."

He was a problem. A big one.

She slammed the door and hurried to the porch. The neighbor's schnauzer barked, as he did every night when she arrived home. Ace's truck lights remained steady while Marisa shoved her key in the lock and slipped inside the house. She switched on the lamp and saw the sweep of headlights across the window as he drove away.

She brushed back the curtain and watched until he turned the corner and disappeared.

What was she going to do about Ace Caldwell?

ACE TRIED to focus on taking care of Marisa's car, but the demon in his brain kept flashing neon signs.

He'd thought he was stronger than this, but Marisa and Chance had chipped away at his progress with their animosity. He didn't want anyone to hate him, certainly not them. Not *her*.

Between Marisa and her brother, he felt about as low as the bottom of his boot, and the desire to numb the hurt threatened to snare him.

He could get her car repaired, but how did a man fix a situation like this one?

He'd passed a liquor store on the return to Sunset Manor. He'd been there plenty of times, knew right where the tequila was shelved. He could stop there on his way out and then head home and to bed. No would be the wiser.

Not a good plan, Ace.

The car first. He'd promised. Then two shots. That would be his limit.

He'd been sober for seventeen months and counting. He could handle a couple of drinks.

Couldn't he?

The night air was cool, but sweat broke out on his upper lip. Sliding into the Toyota seat, too short for his long legs, he tried the starter again, listening to the grind.

His fingers were unsteady against the key fob. Anticipation. Not good.

He reached into his pocket and withdrew a small bronze coin and held it to the dash lights. The token, given to him by his AA brothers, represented one full year without a drink. One year and counting.

He flipped the coin to the back and read the Serenity Prayer, though he'd long ago memorized it. Slowly, the pressure eased. Ace closed his hand, squeezed, and then replaced the coin in his pocket.

As soon as he was done here, he'd head home. Hit the sack. Forget the temptation. That's all it was, a temptation. AA warned about those as well as these moments of vulnerability. A man had to be prepared at all times to wrestle the demon.

He popped the hood to have a look beneath, but before exiting Marisa's vehicle, Ace studied the instrument panel and realized the problem. He gave a satisfied grunt. This, he could fix for her.

Even with the key turned on, the gas gauge registered in the red. Empty. No fuel.

Was she that broke? Or that busy?

Probably both. And still she refused his money. Blood money, she'd called it. A flaming arrow to the chest.

You can pick up those shots on your way to the gas station."Sounds like a plan." The spoken words jarred him. He was talking to the booze. Was he crazy? Did he want to go down that road again?

Not in a million years.

He ripped the cell phone from his pocket and tapped

his brother's ugly mug. On the fifth ring, Nate's groggy voice spoke in his ear. "This better be important."

"It is. I'm in Clay City. Sober. But I could use a brother."

The pause on the other end said Nate was with him. He always had been. "Where are you?"

Ace explained. It was the first time in months he'd been this close to the edge. Would the addiction ever stop sneaking up on him this way?

"I'll be there in twenty. Stay put. Pray. Put on some praise music. Or take a nap. Don't even think about the other."

"Right. Got it." He was ashamed of calling in reinforcements but glad he had, which proved how messed up he was. Still, being proactive gave him more control. He'd make it now. He'd be okay.

Five minutes later, his cell phone mooed. It was Nate. Worry wart of the world, Nate. Everybody's best friend. Especially his.

Nate, the brother who used words sparingly, started a long, chatty conversation as he drove the fifteen miles. He discussed the twins, his wife's miniature animal farm and spring calf prices until his maroon pickup pulled alongside Ace's black one.

A wave of affection and gratitude rose in Ace's chest as he hopped out of his own vehicle and met Nate at the side of the Toyota.

The brawnier brother toted one of the ranch's five gallon gasoline cans.

Relief settled the knot in Ace's neck. "I shouldn't have bothered you."

Nate shrugged him off. "Don't be stupid. Let's get some gas in this baby and get home. I left a warm woman for you. You might be pretty to the ladies, but you can't hold a candle to Whitney."

Ace refused to let him blow off the gratitude. "Seriously, Nate, thank you. I'm sorry."

"I said, shut up." His brother tilted the gas can and jammed the nozzle into the tank. "You drive the Toyota to her house. I'll follow you. Make any stops and I'll kick your tail to China."

"I want to fill the tank on the way."

"All right then. One stop." Nate's gruff voice covered the heart of a teddy bear. "I'm right behind you."

Minutes later, as they stood side by side at the empty, all-night gas station, listening to the pump click, Nate crossed his arms and leaned against the fender.

"You still in love with her?"

The nozzle in Ace's hand jerked. "What? Marisa? No."

At least he hoped not.

"Then why are you letting her get under your skin this way?"

"You know why."

"Making amends is one thing. But if seeing Marisa and Chance pushes you off the wagon, you need to let them go."

Let them go? Now that he'd found them?

"Maybe." But he knew he wouldn't.

MARISA AWAKENED EARLY, her subconscious worrying about the car. What if Ace hadn't gotten it running and she had no ride to work? What if the car needed major repairs? It wasn't as if she'd kept up with the maintenance. In fact, she couldn't remember when she'd had the oil changed. The Toyota had been a dependable friend for years. She'd racked up two hundred thousand miles so far. What if she had to buy a new one? How would she manage that?

The restless nagging pushed her out of the bed into the darkened room. Four-thirty glowed red from the alarm clock. She groaned. Less than five hours of sleep. No wonder she felt like a lead-headed zombie.

To settle the anxiety about the car, she stumbled to the front window and flipped on the porch light.

The Toyota was in the driveway. A white paper gleamed ominously from the windshield. A note. Expecting really bad news, she slipped into her flip flops and went outside.

A chill hung in the air, and she shivered, crossing her arms over her chest. The note was inside the car, propped up against the driver's side windshield.

She tried the door, found it locked, and glanced around the car. What had Ace done with her keys?

After another moment's consideration, she trudged back to the porch and fished inside the mailbox. The key fob rested at the bottom.

Had Ace knocked and tried to rouse her?

She hadn't heard a thing, a chilling concept.

Keys in hand, she unlocked the vehicle, slid inside and peeled the note from the moist glass. It was written on a cattle inventory sheet. *Your car was out of gas. All good now.*

"Oh, for heaven's sake." Marisa couldn't even

remember the last time she'd bought gas. She ran a hand over her sleepy face, relieved and weary of constantly living Murphy's Law. This time, the problem had been of her own making. "What an idiot."

She cranked the starter, and the car responded. The gas gauge climbed to *full,* which could only mean one thing; Ace had filled the tank.

She wanted to maintain her negative attitude toward him, but she was too grateful. At least for this.

On the passenger's seat was a brown paper sack. She hadn't left it, so Ace must have. She peeked inside to discover an array of convenience store foods. Banana, apple, trail mix, a bottle of water, powdered donuts, two granola bars, and a packet of pistachios.

She slowly drew out the pistachios. Had he remembered they were her favorite? Or had this been an accident as he'd grabbed any and everything he could jam inside a brown paper bag?

On the side of the brown sack, he'd scribbled another note in his bold scrawl. "Breakfast. I'll feed you better next time. See you tonight."

A shiver prickled the skin on her arms. Tonight. As if they had a date.

But it wasn't, and even if she wanted it to be, which she did not, Ace's attentions had nothing to do with her and everything to do with Chance.

She traipsed back into her duplex and fell across the bed. The man was messing with her head. Like always.

CHAPTER 6

*A*ce slept late the next morning, comfortably aware that Nate, Gilbert and the ranch hands could run the ranch for a few hours without him. He awoke, unhurried and relaxed, remaining in bed to pray and recommit himself to one more day of sobriety, to being the man God had always intended him to be.

Marisa didn't have the luxury of dawdling.

"What am I supposed to do about her, Lord?"

He was doing everything she'd let him, but it wasn't enough. Dealing with Marisa and Chance was like beating his head against a brick wall. All he got was a headache.

One of the catch phrases from AA ran through his head. *The definition of insanity is doing the same thing and expecting different results.*

He'd done the same thing for weeks. So what could he do differently?

"The million-dollar question," he mumbled as he tossed back the sheet and padded to the shower.

At nine-thirty, showered, shaved and refreshed, he eased into the kitchen for coffee and a talk with the woman who'd raised him. His daddy had hired Consuelo Galindo not long after Ace's mother had passed away from cancer. Ace had been in kindergarten, and his memories of Cori Caldwell were vague at best. Emily and Wyatt had none. Nate more than them all. Most of Ace's memories were of the strong, devout Mexican housekeeper who'd loved him and his siblings and devoted her life to them and the Triple C Ranch. She was his mom, for all practical purposes.

Connie poured two cups of black coffee and set one in front of him. From the work gloves and basket of fresh greens on the counter, she'd already weeded the gardens and picked a batch of baby spinach. The kitchen shone with cleanliness, though the fragrance of bacon still lingered in the air.

"You were out late."

That was Connie. Toss out the question without asking and then sit and wait for the answer. So he explained, leaving out the struggle that forced him to call in the reinforcements.

"You did right. That girl needs you, though she is wounded and stubborn."

"I hurt them both a lot, Connie. There's no repaying that much damage."

"No. But God can heal hearts and give you insight. He will show you what to do."

"I wish he'd hurry."

She wrapped both hands around the white mug, her

dark gaze resting on him, compassionate, loving, and so wise. "Chance still won't talk?"

"No."

"Did you read him the scripture I gave you?"

"I did. Read it two nights in a row."

"Read it again today. Go early. Surprise him. Take something he can't get in that care center. He liked my tamales, yes?"

"Could eat a dozen."

Her white teeth flashed. "Take two dozen. Marisa, she likes them too."

Tamales wouldn't undo the damage, but Ace was desperate enough to try anything.

MARISA WAS thankful for the tank of gas. Really, she was, but she also felt guilty. After her shift at the daycare, she headed home to the duplex, stopping at the corner to pick up her mail from the neighborhood box unit. Mr. Sanchez waved at her from his front porch.

"Need anything from town?" she called. "I have to stop for a few things after work."

"Nothing today."

"Let me know if you change your mind." With a wave, she took the stack of mail and went home.

She only had an hour between jobs, but she kicked off her shoes for a few minutes, grabbed a glass of water and a banana, and plopped on the beige microfiber couch.

She sorted through the mail, tossing advertisements to one side and placing legitimate mail on her lap. The keeper stack was bigger than the junk mail.

Running a finger beneath the flap, she opened each envelope. Except for her bank statement, every piece of mail held a bill of some kind.

The bills came as no surprise but the sheer volume still depressed her. Resolute, she compared her bank statement to her checkbook and began going through her routine, writing out checks for five or ten dollars to each account as if this would somehow whittle down the amounts to zero.

As she opened the final invoice, her heart tumbled. Another medical bill, an astronomical number. This one from months ago. How could she not have known about it?

She slapped the paper against her thigh and tilted her head back onto the couch, eyes closed. The harder she worked, the more behind she became.

"Lord, what am I going to do?" As it had been for months, heaven was silent.

Ace's offer of financial help floated through her thoughts. She rejected it. She'd been on her own all her life. She'd figure this out. Somehow.

TOTING a plastic container and feeling jaunty, Ace tapped in the security code, jerked at the heavy glass door, caught it with his boot, and slipped inside Sunset Manor. He'd been here so often, he'd gotten to know names and called them out or paused for a hello as he traversed the hallway, past walkers and wheelchairs and busy staff members. The smell of fresh hot tamales wafted up like perfume from the plastic container, blotting out the care center odors.

"Watcha got there, cowboy?" Mrs. Reynolds, a sweet lady with a sharp mind whose extreme arthritis confined her to a wheelchair, rolled toward him. So badly twisted and deformed were her joints that she must have been in constant pain, but her pleasant attitude never wavered. A man could take a lesson from this lady.

"Homemade tamales. Want some?" He lofted the box. Connie had sent several dozen.

"No, no. You share them with that sweet Marisa. She could use some meat on those hardworking bones."

So could Mrs. Reynolds, but he kept that thought to himself. "Be glad to if she'll slow down long enough."

The white-haired lady leaned forward in her chair as if to share a confidence. "Are you taking those down to her brother's room?"

"I am."

"Is he talking to you yet?"

Ace wasn't surprised that she knew about Chance's silence. The entire facility must know by now about the fool cowboy who spent several hours a day talking to a man's back and playing cards or chess by himself.

"Not yet."

"So, the tamales are a bribe?"

"Yes, ma'am." He pumped his eyebrows. "Think they'll work?"

Her pleasant smile smoothed a dozen wrinkles. "You're doing a good thing, son. Don't let him discourage you. Either of them. He needs a friend. A real one that won't back off. So does Marisa."

"*She* doesn't think so." Understatement of the year. He

shifted the hot tamale container to his other arm, wondering why he was telling her this.

"Marisa's a good girl, very dedicated to her brother, her job and everyone else except herself. But she doesn't always know what *she* needs."

"Right now that would include less work and more time to eat and relax." Along with ownership of the Denver Mint.

"Exactly." The old woman's hands came together in an almost clap. "See why you're good for her?"

He wouldn't go that far. "Convince her of that."

"I'm working on it." She winked. "Go on, now. Do God's good work."

God's good work. He was here to pay penance, but if God could use him in the process, he was on board.

His step a little lighter, as it always seemed to be after a conversation with Mrs. Reynolds, Ace progressed to Chance's room. The door was open. He paused at the entrance and hefted the container. "Connie sent tamales."

Chance sat in his wheelchair facing him. This time, to Ace's amazement, he didn't turn his back. Chance's shifted to the container and then to Ace. "Why are you doing this?"

At last, they were eye to eye, face to face. Never mind that Chance's expression was as flat as his voice. This was progress.

Even though Chance was too thin, he was still a good looking cuss. Sandy hair, a square jaw and navy blue eyes. Only now, the eyes were dark pools of sadness. Lines bracketed a pinched mouth. Lines of suffering. The once high-energy athlete had lost his sparkle, his verve.

Your fault, the imp in Ace's head whispered.

Yeah, so what else is new?

"Why do you think I'm here?" He kept his tone easy and light, worried the slightest misstep would send Chance retreating into silence.

"My question." The other man's throat convulsed, drawing attention to the pink tracheotomy scar below his Adam's apple. Another reason for Ace to feel responsible. "I saw you last night."

Ace moved deeper into the room, closing the gap but not so close as to look down on his friend. He slid the tamales onto the bedside table. "When?"

"At Marisa's car. Doing what I should have been doing."

Ah, so that was it. Part of it anyway. Chance needed to be the rescuer. He needed to take care of the sister who had always taken care of him. Yet, he couldn't execute the simple task of walking outside to help Marisa get her car back on the road.

Ace swallowed, aching for the other man. "Glad I was around to lend a hand."

Chance's face twisted. "Do you know how it makes me feel not to be able to do anything for her? To be stuck in this room, this chair"— he banged both fists on the wheel-chair arms—"helpless?"

"You're not helpless."

"I was last night."

Ace wouldn't argue about what he couldn't possibly understand. But he felt Chance's despair all the way to his soul.

Heavy with pity he refused to show, Ace grabbed a

nearby chair, spun it close and sat. "She ran out of gas. I happened to be in the parking lot. No big deal."

"I know. I saw Nate arrive with the gas can."

Ace glanced toward the window. The double-wide glass looked out over the parking areas adjacent to the street. He'd never seen the blinds closed. "You don't miss much out that window, do you?"

"Not when it comes to my sister. Watching over her is all I have."

Ace didn't believe that for a second, but this wasn't the time to push.

"We got her fixed up and back on the road."

"Great." Chance turned his head away and stared at the silent TV. "You've done your good deed. You can disappear again."

The accusation jabbed. Ace *had* disappeared. But even though Chance knew about AA, he didn't need to know about the mindless months after the accident when the co-owner of the Triple C Ranch had lived in a stupor.

That was then. This was now.

"Not happening."

"Why? You can't fix my spine. No one can." Chance's words were hard, his glare cold.

Ace had had this conversation with Marisa too many times. It was the insanity thing. Round and round with no new results. The damage to Chance's body might be irreparable, but other paraplegics enjoyed life. Why couldn't Chance?

Ace didn't say that, though he wanted to. He couldn't. Not yet, anyway.

But he would find a way to make a difference in his

friend's life. Somehow. Right now, he was grateful to hear Chance's voice.

He took the lid off the tamale box.

"I can bring an old pal the best tamales in the southwest. Smell that, pal." Ace sucked in a deep, intentionally noisy breath. "Good stuff. Admit it. They smell amazing."

Chance shifted his gaze back to Ace. "I'm glad you were there for her."

"Me, too." He hitched his chin toward the window. "Tell you what. You be the eyes. I'll be the legs. Tell me what she needs, what you think I should do, and I'm there."

Chance narrowed his eyes. "Day or night?"

"Anytime."

Something passed between them, though Ace couldn't say what it was. Understanding maybe. They were two men who cared about the same woman, though in different ways and for different reasons.

Chance's defensive posture eased a smidgen. "I'll think about it." He rolled his chair close to the table laden with tamales. "Connie make these?"

The subject of Marisa was closed. For now. They'd made progress. Ace would have to be satisfied with that.

"She always had a soft spot for you and Marisa."

"Tell her thanks. She makes the best."

If Ace had known tamales would break the ice, he'd have purchased a tamale cart weeks ago.

"Think your sister could find us some plates and forks?"

"No doubt." Chance backed the chair to the bed, reached for the call light and pressed the button.

Marisa charged in, eyes wide and worried, a tigress ready to defend the cub. "What's wrong?" She froze when she saw Ace. "Why are you here so early?"

Ace's heart jumped. He didn't know why, but it did. He suddenly longed to erase Marisa's fear and worry. To pull her close and make all kinds of rash promises.

What was *that* about?

Chance waved away his sister's questions. "Tamales."

Her anxiety shifted to bewilderment. She came deeper into the room, eyes drifting from the container to her brother and then to Ace. "Connie's tamales?"

"The one and only," Ace said. "Want one?"

"Or two or ten." She actually smiled.

Ace smiled back, his pulse doing a two-step. He tried to hold down the thrill, considering that any second now, she might slam him against the wall. Metaphorically speaking. She didn't weigh enough to get physical. But a man could bask in the moment, couldn't he?

"We need plates and forks. Can you hook us up?"

"Now?" She glanced at her watch. "It's not yet dinner time."

Chance made a rude noise. "Lunch wasn't all that inspiring. Tamales are."

Marisa shrugged and left the room. In minutes, she returned with three plates and forks. "Save mine, okay?"

Ace reached for her arm but caught himself before they touched. He let his hand drop. "Stay. Eat with us."

He wasn't ready for her to leave. He wanted more smiles and civil conversation. With her.

"Can't. I just came on duty." She started out, but turned back as if to say something. The words died on her lips when she saw her brother eagerly dishing up a hefty stack of tamales.

For a nano-second, Ace saw the anxiety replaced by loving relief. She mouthed, "Thank you."

Heat expanded in Ace's chest, and it didn't have a thing to do with hot tamales. He didn't need her thanks, but he hoped a wall had crumbled. First, the car, and now, the tamales. Such small things.

A scripture floated through his head, payoff from months of Bible reading. Something about being faithful in little things to prove you can be trusted with bigger ones.

Maybe this was a test.

He sure hoped he passed.

ACE CALDWELL SCARED her to death.

Marisa worked through her shift in a daze, changing beds, assisting residents, and maintaining a friendly demeanor while her mind whirled with one thing. Or rather, one person. Ace Caldwell. As much as she wanted to, she couldn't deny the tug of attraction that simply would not go away.

She'd loved him. Desperately. And desperate was never a good thing in a relationship. Her mother had been the same with her father, falling into the alcohol with her dad until both parents had ended up on skid row while their kids grew up in foster care. That was not the life for Marisa.

Yet, the cowboy who'd broken her heart seemed to have changed. He'd always been charming and thoughtful, but not like this. In the past, his charm and thoughtfulness had come with an agenda. This Ace Caldwell seemed so different. Humble, broken, and determined to set things right.

The Lord *could* change people. She knew that, had seen it in others, including herself all those years ago when she'd been a foster teen with a massive chip on her shoulder.

But what if she was wrong about him? She'd been fooled before. What if Ace hadn't changed? She'd once trusted him with her brother, and it had cost them both too much. She couldn't bear for Chance to suffer any more.

Yet, hadn't Jesus said something about forgiving seven times seventy if the guilty party repented of his sins?

Ace had repented. He'd apologized. He'd taken the blame.

A nagging voice tried to interrupt, to make her recall the facts about the accident. She didn't want to think about that night. Ever. Regardless of who had been behind the wheel of that truck, Ace was responsible for Chance's accident.

She *had* forgiven him. But she didn't trust him. Or herself. How could she?

A battle raged in her head and, more than once during her shift, she forgot what she was doing. When the charge nurse asked for the third time if she was sick and offered a fifteen-minute break, Marisa gratefully accepted.

She headed straight for Chance's room. What she observed there amazed her. He was interacting, talking, listening. The belligerent, hopeless attitude had lessened.

She didn't know what Ace had done to break through the funk—she couldn't credit the tamales with everything—but she was thankful.

The smell of those tamales tempted her almost as much as Ace did. Or once had.

She swept into the room, her perky expression in place. Chance was never fooled, but she kept up the charade that everything in her world was perfect. The bills were her problem. Her brother had enough to deal with.

Ace's back was to the door, but Chance saw her and said, "Quick, the tamales. Feed her before she perishes."

Chance joking? This was a rare event indeed.

She stuck out an arm. "Intravenously."

Ace twisted in the chair and smiled. Oh, that smile, half crooked-sexy and half orthodontist's dream. "Rough day so far?"

"Busy. My head's not in the game for some reason."

Part of that reason, a lean, green-eyed cowboy, rose and offered his chair. "Sit. You had a rough night last night."

On principal, she should have refused, but the early morning and busy shift were taking a toll on her energy level. She sat. "Which brings us to my car. I didn't thank you properly."

He pushed a plate of tamales toward her. "Eat these and consider your debt paid in full."

She reached for the fork, waved it. "What a deal. I'll take it."

"We can warm those up if they're too cold."

"Hot tamales are never too cold." She took a bite and moaned in approval.

"As good as you remember?" A soft, pleased smile played around the edges of his mouth. Another thing she remembered about him. He was the best kisser.

Nope. Not heading in that direction.

Eyes averted from that memorable mouth, she chewed, appreciated, swallowed. "Better."

"Chance said the same thing. Connie will be thrilled. You know how she loves to feed people." He hovered over the tamales, close to her plate, close to her. She could feel his watchful gaze. "Prepare yourself. More food will come. I can't stop her."

Marisa almost laughed. Instead, she shoved in another bite.

Ace spooned a second tamale onto her plate and then retreated to the wall. In a room this small, three people was a crowd. "You're taking the leftovers home with you."

Chance squawked. "No, she's not. They're staying here. I'm eating all of them. Probably tonight."

It was the first time in months she'd seen this teasing side of her brother. The person who deserved the credit was Ace, whether she liked admitting it or not.

She tugged the still-packed box of tamales to her side of the table. "Sharing is the right thing to do, little brother."

Chance pulled the box back, his grin wicked with humor. "Then share."

Marisa was so pleased by her brother's improved mood, she pretended capitulation. "All right. You win. But don't eat them all, and we'll do this again tomorrow."

"Can't make any promise, but I'll try to restrain myself."

Marisa grinned, pushed the plate aside and glanced at her watch. "Break time goes faster than any other part of the day. Do you need anything before I get back to my job?"

Ace shoved away from the wall. "I think I'll grab a cup of coffee. How about you, Chance?"

"Coke, maybe?"

"You got it." Ace followed Marisa out into the hall. "Do you have a minute?"

Marisa paused, warning alarms going off inside. "What?"

"We need to talk. When do you have another day off?"

"I thought your private detective told you everything about us."

"Not everything." Her snarky attitude didn't seem to bother him. "So, when do you have time off this week?"

"Thursday." She shifted, blew out a breath, and said the meanest thing she could think of. "I don't have anything to say to you, Ace. I tolerate your visits, but we are not friends."

Again, he didn't let her bad attitude get to him. "Chance seemed almost happy tonight, didn't he?"

Grudgingly, Marisa had to admit he did. "I haven't seen him like that since we moved back to Clay City."

"I'm not taking credit for it, but I have ideas, ways to get him interested in the world again. Will you meet me? Hear me out?"

"We did that already."

"That was a preliminary meeting with each of us

dancing around the other like championship boxers. We accomplished exactly nothing and neither has Chance. He needs a boost, and we can give him that."

The battle fired up, raging again. She didn't trust this cowboy and didn't trust herself around him. But he wasn't asking to be with her. He was asking for her brother's benefit. Chance had always been her weak spot, her Kryptonite, and Ace knew it.

She glanced at a light over one of the resident's rooms. It had just come on. A reprieve. "I have to go, lights to answer."

He caught her upper arm. "Thursday. Okay? You pick the time and place."

Marisa glanced down at his long fingers wrapped around her much smaller biceps. Holding her tenderly, lightly, the way he used to hold all of her, as if she were fragile. As if he cared. "I'll think about it."

Clear, green eyes searched hers, tugged at her, and made her wish for things she shouldn't. Made her remember the good times, the laughs, the love.

"Fair enough." He loosened his grip.

Marisa hurried away without looking back. The memory of Ace's warm touch went with her.

CHAPTER 7

"I hate this place."

"This particular place? Or any place that confines you to a wheelchair?"

Ace was in Chance's room as he was at least four nights a week. Arms folded across his chest, and ankles crossed as he leaned against the wall at the end of Chance's bed, he eyed the younger man with pretend calm.

The last three days had been good ones, even if Marisa still refused to meet with him.

But tonight, Chance was in one of his moods. A really rotten mood. Marisa had warned Ace the minute he'd stepped inside the building about a bad round with physical therapy. She'd rested a hand on his arm, and he'd been fool enough to hope that single touch meant something.

"Both," Chance said. "I hate this place. I hate this chair. I hate my life."

The pity Ace had felt from the beginning was waning

fast. Chance didn't need pity. He needed a good, cowboy kick-start.

But was the man who was instrumental in putting him in that wheelchair the right person to give it? Probably not, but Ace was the only one here.

He uncrossed his ankles and moved closer to the bed. "Then stop whining and do something about it."

Chance's nostrils flared in annoyance. "Yeah, right. Good advice, Caldwell."

"Seriously. Get your act together and get out of here, run your own life."

"In case you haven't noticed, wise guy, I'm paralyzed. I can't *run* anywhere. Ever again."

"That's not your biggest problem."

"What would you know about it? You have two good legs."

"Other paraplegics live full lives."

"Good for them."

Ace whipped out his cell phone and did a quick search. He'd been waiting for this moment. In view of the current negative attitude from Chance, Ace figured he couldn't make things worse by trying something new.

When he found what he was looking for, he handed the device to Chance. "Watch this."

Sullenly, Chance watched the video. As he did, his expression changed. Slowly, his interest piqued. When the video ended, he said, "There probably aren't many paras in such good shape."

The videos showed paraplegics participating in a variety of activities, everything from skiing to tennis. "Want to bet a burger on that?"

Marisa sailed into the room. "No betting in this establishment."

Every nerve in Ace's body reacted. Even an exhausted, skinny Marisa in baggy scrubs made his blood hum and his world brighter. "That's because you've already won all my toothpicks in poker."

She flashed him a smile, and he answered with one of his own. He credited the tamales. Times like this, he almost believed she liked him again.

"What are you two outlaws betting on?"

Ace took the phone from Chance and handed it to Marisa. She watched with interest before saying, "The docs and therapists have told him this kind of lifestyle is possible, but I think it's too dangerous. What if he gets hurt?"

"What if he doesn't?"

"No." She shook her head, her lips thinning. "It's too risky. I will never allow him to be put in danger again."

He heard what she didn't say but was likely thinking. Ace had put them both at risk the night of Chance's birthday, and the results had been tragic.

How did he convince her he was not that guy? That, through Christ, he was a new man? Not that his sober life would change Chance's situation.

Jesus had forgiven him. Would Marisa ever be able to?

"Proposition. Pick a day when you don't work, and I'll take both of you out to the ranch. Fresh air, fishing, Connie's cooking." He pivoted toward Chance. "What do you think, Chance? The decision is yours."

Before the younger man could speak, Marisa exploded. "Absolutely not. No. Just...no."

"Why not? The ranch is as safe and harmless as any place you'll find."

"I said no, Ace. And that's that."

She spun like a tornado and blew out of the room.

Chance made a low humming sound. "You put her knickers in a twist."

Ace turned to face his friend. "Sorry about that."

"I thought going out to your ranch was a great idea."

"No kidding?"

"Anything to get out of here for a day."

"She's afraid for you."

"Controlling, overprotective, scared to death. But without her, I'd be toast."

"She's a good woman. And she loves you a lot."

"To the point of sacrificing everything for me. I've studied enough psychology to know that's not good for either of us. She needs to find a good man, get married, and have ten kids to fuss over."

"Is she going out with anyone?" Ace kept the tone casual, but he listened intently. He'd loved her once. He didn't want some jerk of a guy messing with her.

Chance gave him a long look. "Not since you."

The admission struck Ace in the chest. She'd loved him. He'd devastated her. Now, she hated him. And she was alone in this fight to care for her brother.

Chance levered up. "Help me out of this bed, would you?"

Glad for the change of topics, Ace grabbed the wheel-chair and unfolded it. "Tell me what to do."

Under Chance's instructions, Ace easily helped him into his chair. He was strong and fit, and Chance had lost a lot of weight. "You're not near as hard to wrestle as a steer."

Chance flexed a puny arm. "Weak as a baby."

"You could use some upper body weights to get back in shape."

"Yeah. They've got some here. Baby weights. I never go down to the fitness room. It's useless."

Chance settled into the chair. He adjusted, poked a pillow behind his back and lifted each bare foot onto the foot rest with his hands.

Ace watched the movement, stricken by the flaccid muscles in the athletic man's lower body. He'd once been more physically fit than Ace, a coach and a ball player, always active.

Chance must have read his expression because he stilled, hands around his upper thigh. "It wasn't your fault, Ace."

Grief welled up in Ace's chest, gripping his heart in an iron fist. "Yes, it was."

"I was twenty-four years old, not a kid. I made my own stupid choices that night."

"My truck. My keys." Ace's throat constricted. He swallowed past the ache. "I shouldn't have asked you to drive."

"I thought I was sober enough. You certainly weren't."

"Neither of us was." Ace didn't remember much of anything past handing the keys to Chance inside the bar. At some point later, he'd crawled into the back seat of the truck and passed out. He'd awoken to the sound of sirens. Lots and lots of sirens.

"I wanted to blame you, but I can't. I took your keys."

Chance reached for a plastic water cup. His fingers trembled. "You didn't force me to drink that night."

"I bought a few rounds."

"And I bought a few more." Chance paused to sip at the cup. "If you'd been the one who was badly injured, would you have blamed me?"

Ace dragged a hand over his face, considering. "No man can say how he'd feel about something like that until it happens to him. I hope I wouldn't."

"You wouldn't. You're not made that way. But us Foremans come from dysfunctional parents with victim mentalities. Marisa and I used to discuss it." He made a face. "Lately, we don't discuss anything, but back then, when I was in college, we promised not to be like our parents. They blame something or someone for every bad thing that happens to them, when most is their own fault. A lost job was because of a mean boss, not the fact that they'd missed days of work while they binged. Losing their kids? A broken system. Getting tossed in jail for public drunk or breaking into a vacant house? Police were bullies. They expect the world to give them a break no matter what they do. Marisa and I promised not to be that way. We'd fight our way out of the pit and be better."

"And you did."

"Did we?"

Ace rested a hand on his friend's shoulder. "In AA we talk about changing the things we can and accepting the things we can't. I think it applies in your case, too."

"Yeah. Maybe." Chance wheeled his chair toward the door and closed it. He swiveled back toward Ace with a sneaky grin. "When are we going fishing?"

Ace held up both hands, palms out. "We have to convince your sister first."

"I don't need her permission, Ace."

"Maybe not, but I do." He'd done enough to hurt her. He wouldn't intentionally do more.

And getting her approval would not be an easy task.

MARISA HEARD the laughter long before she got to Chance's room. Ace was there again.

For the last five days, ever since tamale night, he and Chance had behaved as if nothing bad had ever happened between them. It made her nervous. Ace made her nervous. Probably because hearing his voice and seeing him again had her wishing things had turned out differently, and not just for her brother. She understood the psychology, but knowing her predilection for men like Ace didn't stop her silly heart from overreacting every time she thought of him.

Still, he was exactly the reason she'd arrived an hour early today. Saturday was her day off from daycare, and her errands were finished. She wanted time with her brother alone. She hadn't known Ace would be here.

Another burst of laughter caught her as she whisked inside the utilitarian room.

Ace looked up, affecting a jiggle in her pulse as he motioned to her. "Come here. You gotta see this."

An iPad was propped on Chance's rolling table, and her brother was glued to the screen. Suddenly, he cackled and rocked back in his chair. The movement shifted his paralyzed body to one side, unbalancing him.

"Chance!" Alarmed, Marisa rushed to him, bracing his body and the chair with her side. "Be careful. You'll fall. You know what happened before."

Chance's laugher died. "That was months ago."

"But the fall set you back. You can't afford to have that happen again."

Chance closed his eyes and sighed.

The atmosphere in the room palled. Was it her fault? Had she embarrassed her brother in front of company? Surely, he didn't care what Ace thought.

She searched for a way to elevate the mood.

"What were you guys laughing about when I came in? Must have been hysterical."

Chance didn't open his eyes. "Nothing."

"Oh, come on, pal, cut her some slack. She can't help being a control freak."

Marisa bristled. "I am not."

"Sure, you are." Ace swirled the iPad in her direction. "We're watching funny YouTube videos. Pull up a chair."

"I can't."

Ignoring her protest, Ace dragged the chair closer to the small screen. A cat skittered across the video, all four feet stretched across a bathroom doorway in determined resistance. He did not want a bath.

Marisa grinned. The next animal video appeared, and she laughed. Standing next to her, close enough that she could feel his body heat, Ace laughed too.

Chance's curiosity must have overcome his aggravation because he laughed at the third one. Marisa snuck a glance at Ace. He winked but didn't remark on the change in her brother.

Her pulse did the jiggle thing again, and this time she let it. As long as she knew the score, what did it matter if she reacted to an attractive man?

There was the problem. She'd not been on a date since the breakup with Ace. Between Chance's injury and work, she'd had no time or interest. Didn't matter now. What man would want a woman who came with a grown brother to care for the rest of his life?

Horrified at the turn of thoughts, she slipped out of the room, away from the two men who were driving her crazy.

CITY PARK WOULDN'T HAVE BEEN his first choice, but when Marisa finally consented to meet him, Ace readily agreed to her terms.

He also stopped off at the nearest pizza parlor for a large Canadian bacon pizza, cinnamon bread sticks, and root beer. Marisa, he recalled, loved all three.

He waited for her at the entrance, a sidewalk that led into Clay City's pretty park of massive old trees and concrete picnic tables. Up the hill from the tables was the local swimming pool, empty now until school dismissed for summer. To the left near the restrooms and drinking fountain, a large wooden play town hosted a handful of giggling, squealing preschoolers and their moms. One lone dad in baggy shorts and a ball cap pushed a little girl in a swing while she called, "Higher, Daddy, higher."

Kids. He wanted a few. At one time, he'd thought of marriage and family as something in the distant future, but lately he yearned for what his brother and sister had—

a steady, solid love with the right person and a couple of kids. The desire to settle would stun his siblings if they knew.

Maybe God was changing him in more ways than one.

An older model red Toyota pulled up and parked beside his truck. Marisa, in jeans and a pale blue T-shirt, got out. Her dark, thick hair was pulled back at the nape into a single braid, one of those fancy things that twisted along the sides and met in the back. A rope he could braid, but the fancy hair braids baffled him. He liked it though. She looked fresh, pretty, and young, her shirt color emphasizing the blue in her gray eyes.

She licked her lips and swallowed. Those pretty eyes shifted away.

The once natural ease of their relationship had disappeared in the aftermath of the accident.

His fault. Again.

"Hey." He stepped toward her. "I'm glad you came."

Too glad, if the grasshoppers jumping in his belly were any indication.

Marisa saw the pizza and relaxed a little. "Softening me up?"

"Bread sticks." He lofted the soda. "And root beer."

"All this? After the tamales?" She reached for the bread stick box and sniffed in appreciation. "Cinnamon. Mmm. Must be true what they say. The way to a woman's heart—"

She caught herself and stopped, her expression flattening.

Ace bumped her shoulder with his. "Lighten up. You were joking. Joking is good."

He *was* softening her up, and even if he wanted to win her heart again, he wasn't dumb enough to think it would be as easy as tamales and pizza.

As they walked side by side toward a shady table, he pondered the mix of emotions Marisa engendered. Exasperation. Compassion. Grief and guilt. But there was more too. Truth was, he'd never settled the Marisa issue.

They reached the table and deposited the boxes. Marisa took the bench on one side, and he sat on the other. Scattered sunlight filtered through the tall, leafy trees and dappled the table and them. For once, the Oklahoma breeze was light, so the paper napkins didn't blow away.

He flipped open the cardboard box and held the pizza toward her. "Canadian bacon."

"You dog. You don't play fair."

He laughed. She was teasing him. The Marisa he'd loved was finally sitting across from him without an expression of censure.

It hit him then. He'd missed her.

Marisa took a pizza slice, the hot cheese stringing behind. She slid a finger underneath and broke it off.

Ace waited, hoping she'd do what she once had.

She didn't.

Sad for reasons that made no sense, he chose a slice. "I'll ask the blessing."

Her gaze was solemn, questioning, as he bowed his head and murmured a simple prayer. He could practically read her thoughts. Was he for real? Or was this an act concocted to get his way?

Actions, Connie had taught him, speak louder than

words. For too long, his actions had screamed selfishness, and only new actions could prove that he'd turned a corner.

He chowed down on the still hot pizza. They ate in silence for a few minutes, focused on the lunch and the park.

"It's a pretty day for a picnic. I'm glad you brought food."

"I always think of food. It's the Caldwell way of relating."

"I seem to recall all those Sunday dinners, cookouts for random reasons, birthday parties. Do you still do that?"

It had been only a couple of years since she'd been to the ranch, not a lifetime, but he knew better than to say that. "Every chance we get. We had a birthday party for Nate's twins a few weeks ago, and Connie is already itching to fire up the smoker again."

"Sounds like fun."

"Want to come?" He tossed the question out as casually as he could.

"You know I can't."

"I *don't* know that. You need a break and time to relax with people who like you." And he really wanted her to say yes.

"I like them, too. You have a great family." The words were wistful.

His heart jumped. She'd had so little in the way of familial relationships. She and Chance against the world.

"Then come." He put aside his half-eaten pizza slice and leaned in. "Take a day off."

"I haven't worked at either job long enough to receive paid leave."

He wanted to say he'd pay her, but she'd take it the wrong way, and they'd be back to square one.

He couldn't take the chance. The last few times he'd seen her, she hadn't seemed so angry, and Ace thought they were gaining ground. She'd started hanging out longer to talk, mostly about nothing important, but the conversation was friendly and kept Chance entertained. As long as the accident wasn't mentioned, she didn't seem to despise him quite as much.

"Then we'll plan something on your regular day off."

She cocked her head, stared at him. "Why would you do that?"

"Now that Emily is married with a baby, Nate is married with twins, and Wyatt rarely comes home, I'm the odd man out." He wasn't, but it sounded like a good argument.

"So take a date."

"Not interested."

She looked up. "What?"

Maybe he shouldn't have offered that personal bit of information. He didn't want to discuss the indiscriminate binge months followed by the ugly battle with a very personal demon. He had no time or energy left for dates.

As an excuse not to discuss his love life, Ace grabbed a napkin and reached across the table. "You've got sauce—"

A speck of marinara lingered on Marisa's right cheek, close to her mouth. That beautiful, kissable mouth. Soft and firm at the same time, supple and sweet.

He held her chin to wipe away the marinara. Her

breath made warm puffs against his skin. His arm hair prickled in response.

He didn't know if he was thankful for the table between them or if he wanted to jump across it and take her in his arms.

Yeah. *That.*

He'd give a hundred dollars to kiss her again. Make that a thousand.

He hadn't been with a woman since starting AA. Marisa was the reason, though he'd not realized it until now.

She watched him, quiet as the breeze, but he felt the uptick in her breathing. Did he still affect her as much as she affected him? Or was he imagining her response because he wanted it?

Ace sat back, aware his heart was galloping. His goal was to make amends, not restart a relationship that could never be the same. Even if a sober Ace didn't find anyone else the slightest bit appealing.

"Want more pizza?" He pushed the box toward Marisa.

She took another slice. This time, she meticulously picked away the mushrooms. Ace offered an open palm. Lips curved, she placed the offending mushrooms in his hand. He dumped them onto his next piece the way he'd done when they were a couple.

What had changed?

"Still hate them?"

She offered a fake shudder. "Squishy, nasty things."

"All the more for me." Ace felt light and happy, a dumb reaction to a handful of cooked mushrooms.

He popped one in his mouth, chewed and swallowed,

then swigged root beer to wash down an unexpected surge of longing. "Chance needs to get out of that place."

He hadn't intended to be quite that abrupt.

Marisa bristled. "*That place* is the best facility around."

Ace raised a hand in surrender. "I wasn't criticizing. Sunset Manor is a good place. For elders. Chance is a young, vital man. He needs to go places, do things, and get involved in life again."

"We've had this discussion, Ace. He won't."

And you won't let him. You object until he gives in, not wanting to upset you.

"He does this time. He wants to come to the ranch. He told me so."

She was already shaking her head. "The answer was no before, and it's still no. A ranch is too dangerous. He could get hurt."

It was always that. Her fear of injury. *Her* fear, not Chance's.

"I'll be with him. I won't let anything bad happen."

The words fell between them like boulders. He'd let something bad happen before.

"He needs this, Marisa. It's all he talks about."

"You went behind my back after I told you how I felt?"

"He's excited about something. Isn't that progress?" Ace leaned closer, itching to touch her again. "If you can't trust me, trust my family. Plus, you'll be with him every minute."

She went silent, her lips drawn down and set in stubborn refusal. The pizza slice hung limp from her hand.

Chance didn't need her permission to do anything, but telling that to Marisa would instigate World War III.

Frustrated, Ace left the table to toss his empty soda can into a trash receptacle. Aluminum rattled against the metal barrel. Honey bees swarmed up from the smelly garbage, buzzed a few seconds while Ace prepared to run, and then settled again.

Marisa rose too. To his utter shock, she placed a hand on his shoulder.

Voice kind, she said, "I know you're trying to help him, Ace. I see what you're doing, how hard you're trying, and I appreciate the efforts, but a wheelchair and the care center are his life now."

Ace's hands closed into fists. "I don't accept that. Giving up is failure."

"You told me you wanted to make amends for what happened. You've succeeded. You're sorry. We get it. But this is as far as it can go."

"But Chance—"

"I don't want him filled with false hopes that will only bring him more grief. He's had too many of those. With every failure and setback, his depression deepens, and he retreats into himself. Sometimes, I'm scared he'll withdraw until I lose him forever."

Ace covered her hand with his and drew it to his chest. She didn't yank away or slap his face. He wasn't sure why, but he wasn't about to question his good fortune.

"He worries about you, too, Marisa, and feels rotten because your world revolves around his disability. He says he's stolen your life."

"There's nothing either of us can do about that. He's my brother, and I will always take care of him. If I could, I'd bring him home and care for him twenty-four-seven."

But she couldn't. Marisa had to work, and there was no one else to look after her brother. "What if we hired someone to be with him while you're at work?"

"Can't afford it." She pointed at him. "And before you say any more, the answer is no. I won't let you."

"You're a frustratingly independent woman, you know that?"

"You've said that to me a few times. You used to admire it."

"Still do. Just not in this case." She was wrong, and her stubbornness was making life harder for her brother.

Marisa made a face. "You're such a guy."

"Guilty." He laced his fingers with hers and lifted their hands together to point toward the playground. "Want to swing?"

"Seriously?"

"We're here. The pizza is pretty much gone. Bread sticks are cold." And I've fired all my argument arrows without hitting a single bullseye. "Let's get some exercise."

He'd already started in the direction of the swings and was glad when she came along without a struggle.

He was going to find a way to help her and Chance. But right now, he was going to do some more softening up.

MARISA HADN'T LAUGHED this much in months. Not since before—

She froze the thought and locked it away. For the first time in forever, she was having harmless fun, and she refused to spoil the sunny afternoon with bad memories. This wasn't a date. It wasn't a relationship. She could leave anytime she wanted to. Except she didn't want to.

Once Ace stopped talking about Chance visiting the ranch, the laughs had begun. She probably should have been a little suspicious at how easily he'd capitulated. The Ace she knew didn't give up.

They were on the swings. Ace had given her a push, teasing her to pump like a ten-year-old, and then he'd hopped into the swing next to her.

He'd joked, making silly comments about everything and kept the chatter so light, she didn't feel the least bit uncomfortable. He was the charming Ace of old. Except he wasn't.

If she didn't know what she knew, she'd like this new Ace even more than the old one.

Right now, he looked ridiculous, his long, cowboy-booted legs jutting out from a child's swing. He'd jammed his hat down so tightly, his forehead disappeared, and she could barely see his eyes.

She pointed, snorting.

He tilted his face up and peered from beneath the hat brim. With a goofy expression, he asked, "Are you laughing at me?"

She giggled. *Giggled* like a teenager. When was the last time she'd done *that*? "Not at you. With you."

"That's what they all say." As if determined to make her laugh more, he stood up in the seat, a flimsy rubber device that sagged with pressure. "Watch this."

He wobbled, unbalanced for a few seconds, and looked ridiculous and adorable, two words she'd never have associated with this prideful, macho cowboy. She wanted to hug him.

The swing began its back and forth motion. Slowly.

"I'm watching. Not impressed." But she was grinning like a little kid.

He rocked his long, lean body and shot her a wounded look. "What did you expect? Cirque du Soleil?"

"Something like that. Dazzle me with your mad skills."

"Okay, how about this great balancing act?" He lofted a boot to stand on one foot like a flamingo. The flaccid rubber seat shifted. The chains wobbled wildly. His boot slipped.

And Ace tumbled out, landing hard on his backside.

Marisa leaped from her swing and squatted next to him. She couldn't stop the laugh that bubbled up. "Are you hurt?"

He gave a wry grin. "Would you kiss it and make it better if I were?"

"Considering how you landed, that would be a no."

He tipped his hat back and pumped a pair of wicked eyebrows. "What if I'd landed on my pretty face?"

Oh, the temptation. But he laughed, and she laughed with him.

Heart light, happy and playful in a way she hadn't been in months, Marisa tapped his cheek. "We'll never know, will we?"

"Now, there's a challenge if I ever heard one." Ace reached out, hooked her neck with an elbow and plopped her onto his lap.

She landed against his chest with a laugh and an *oof*. He felt familiar, muscles firm and strong from ranch work, his body warm and welcoming. Marisa didn't want to notice, but she did. And worse, she liked being this close to him.

Ace looped a loose arm around her waist and held her, saying nothing, relaxed, his chest rising and falling in easy breaths. She leaned against his heart, soothed and oddly content.

She expected him to do something to upset her, something that would break the spell of his nearness and, more than that, his sweetness. But when he didn't slide a hand under her shirt or kiss her neck, she relaxed and listened to his solid, steady heartbeat.

Memories of the good times flooded in. Of the times she'd mourned her alcoholic parents, and Ace had been there to hold her. Times they'd discussed the future and children and hinted at forever. Of weekends at the Triple C with his amazing family. Then there was the week she'd had the stomach flu, and Ace had slept on her couch, getting up all through the nights to tend her. No one else had ever done that. No one.

A paradigm shifted. The universe came into clear focus.

Ace hadn't been an ogre.

Marisa squeezed her eyes shut and ached for what was lost. For Chance, of course, but also for herself and Ace.

he Sunday dinner table at the Triple C Ranch was not only a tradition, it was a mandate. Every available Caldwell must attend, along with any guests they wanted to bring. And there were almost always guests.

Lively conversation filled the big dining room. Dishes clinked and chairs scraped. One of Nate and Whitney's twins, Olivia, chattered nonstop from her booster chair next to Connie. She only hushed when Connie handed her a pickle.

Ace passed one of two massive roast beef platters to his left. Grass-fed Triple C beef, of course.

Today's table included the usual suspects: Nate, Whitney and the into-everything twins. Emily and Levi with nine-month-old Mason napping in the crib upstairs. And of course, Connie and Gilbert.

What made today special was the addition of the youngest brother, Wyatt, home on leave from the military.

Even out of uniform, he looked like a soldier, posture perfect, muscles curved and firm beneath a white T-shirt and a short military haircut.

"Where do you go next, Wyatt?" Emily took a helping of salad and passed the bowl to her husband.

Of the siblings, Ace and Emily looked the most like their mother with black hair and green eyes. Nate was brawnier with Dad's lighter hair and brown eyes. Wyatt looked like no one else, and he'd taken plenty of ribbing because of it.

The blue eyed, sandy-haired soldier forked a roasted potato and studied it as if searching for a concealed listening device. "No orders yet. For now, back to the base."

He jammed the potato into his mouth and chewed. The update was all they'd learn about his military work. As a specialist in cyber intelligence, Wyatt was involved in security operations he wouldn't or couldn't discuss.

Ace thought his baby brother seemed a little more intense than usual but blew off the concern. Scary smart and a perfectionist, Wyatt had been born intense.

A cry sounded from upstairs, and Emily bolted, nearly knocking over her tea glass. Levi caught the glass and followed her up from the table. "I'll get him, Em. Finish your dinner."

"No, I'll do it. You should eat." Emily left the dining room.

Levi wagged his head and followed, muttering, "Stubborn woman."

Ace understood the sentiment. Marisa was the same.

He wished she'd agreed to come today. He'd asked. More than once.

Before Ace knew exactly what he wanted to say, he spoke. "I need some advice."

Asking for help was one of the lessons he was learning in AA. He'd never been good at that.

Except for the twins, the table quieted. All heads turned in his direction.

"Are you okay?" This from Connie whose black eyes had grown wide and worried. "You've been gone a lot lately."

"To see Marisa and Chance. That's all, Connie. I'm good."

He knew what concerned her. She worried he was drinking again. It hurt to know his family, even loyal, loving Connie who'd fight a bear for him, still feared he'd fall back into the abyss.

"He's handling it, Connie. Stop worrying." Nate met Ace's gaze across an ocean of home-cooked food. The memory of that late night phone call hung between them, private and secure.

The whole family kept a close eye on him, though to their credit, they were subtle about it. After they'd dragged him kicking and screaming out of his stupor, he couldn't blame them.

"Chance is stuck in that wheelchair and Marisa is scared to let him do anything." He explained the situation, right down to his offer of a day at the ranch.

Emily and Levi reentered the dining room. Against one shoulder, Levi toted a sleepy-eyed Mason, the baby they'd adopted when Levi's brother and sister-in-law had died in a flash flood. Emily walked close to her husband, her hand at his back, eyes sparkling with love.

Ace was happy for his sister's newfound joy, but he was envious too.

"Why wouldn't she agree?" Emily took a seat and pulled the baby from her husband onto her lap, looping both hands around Mason's waist. "She likes us. We like her."

"Other than the fact that she blames me for the accident?"

"Blame does no one any good. You are praying, *si?*"

"So much I think God's getting an earache."

Whitney, quiet until now, lifted a wiggling Sophia from the booster chair to the floor. "I suspect she's afraid, Ace. Afraid of making the wrong decisions and causing her brother more harm. Afraid of trusting you or anyone, because no one has ever been there for her. That's a scary thing."

Nate put an arm around his wife, his gaze tender. "You're not alone anymore, babe."

She patted his big hand and snuggled closer. "Thanks to you. But Marisa is."

Whitney had been worse than alone. She'd been homeless and struggling to raise her babies. If anyone could relate to Marisa, she could.

Ace mulled the conversation, grateful for their encouragement. He had the best family in the world. Marisa had no one.

"Maybe she's worried about accessibility." Nate glanced around the room, spacious, but crowded with people and furniture. "The ranch isn't exactly set up for a wheelchair. Even the front steps would be a problem."

"We could fix it." Gilbert, the Seminole Indian who was more uncle than ranch hand, reached for another hot roll. "You and me, we've built ramps before."

"Our doorways are plenty wide," Connie added.

"We can make it happen." Nate spooned more gravy over his roast. "I have some time next week. You, Gilbert?"

"I can squeeze in a few hours."

Love filled Ace's chest. Every person at this table had his back.

Connie waved a fork filled with roasted carrot. "A ramp would be good to have for the future. I will get old soon and need it."

The four siblings glared at Connie. Ace pointed a finger and spoke for all of them. "No. You won't. It's not allowed. But we can still build the ramp."

Connie laughed and clapped her hands. "*Bueno*. When it is built, I will talk to Marisa. She will come."

MARISA DIDN'T KNOW whether to be angry or scared to death. Maybe both. She put a hand to her jittery belly. A little part of her was excited too. Other than the afternoon in the park, she hadn't been anywhere or done anything for pleasure since the accident. She'd been too consumed with Chance's care.

She was in her brother's room, preparing for a day at the Triple C Ranch. Fidgety, uncertain, and worried she'd forget something important, she removed every item from her tote bag.

"That's the third time, sis." Chance's voice was gentle and slightly amused. "Stop fretting. Everything will be okay."

"I don't know how I let myself get talked into this." But she did know. Ace Caldwell did not play fair. He'd sicced Connie on her.

"Connie has super powers. Gotta love her."

Connie, in her gentle, frank manner, had proved relentless. When she'd pulled the, "where is your faith, little one? God has not given us the spirit of fear," Marisa had capitulated.

Now she wasn't so sure, but Chance had been blatantly clear. He was going fishing with Ace, with or without her, which left her no real choice at all. She had to go. The last time Chance had gone off with Ace had been too disastrous to forget.

Tossing a can of bug spray into the tote, Marisa watched her little brother. Today was the first time he'd wanted to go anywhere since the accident.

Chance rolled his chair to the closet and took out a pair of athletic shoes. "Wonder if these still fit?"

The question pinched Marisa's heart. She took the shoes and slid them onto his feet, tying them with a cheerful flourish. "Perfect as always."

Before the accident, he'd been into athletic shoes, buying a pair for every sport he played or coached, and that was several. Since he now wore whatever anyone stuck on his feet—mostly socks or house slippers—he had no use for his closetful of shoes.

The pain of that reminder was a chainsaw through the soul. The gifted athlete would never walk or run again.

For once, the rage against Ace didn't come. She wanted it to, but the recent memories of his efforts on her behalf, and the way he'd held her at the park, overrode the anger. In truth, anger had become exhausting to sustain.

She'd always been a sucker for Ace Caldwell. Was she doing it again? Was she leading her brother back into the lion's den? Was she like her mother, after all?

Chance wheeled to the window, the chair whispering against the tile, and gazed out. His fingers tapped restlessly on the padded arm, his body alert and watchful.

"What time will Ace be here?"

She glanced at her watch. "Any minute."

Chance was excited. For that she was grateful, even though her misgivings wouldn't go away. A day at the ranch sounded harmless enough, but she knew her brother and she knew Ace. They were athletes, daredevils, eager to push the envelope and try things. Ace had once convinced Chance to ride a steer, and they'd thought the resulting video was the funniest thing in the world. If she didn't keep a close eye on them, they'd be doing something dangerous.

Even if they didn't, dangers abounded at a ranch.

Connie promised that no alcohol was allowed anywhere on the Triple C and that Ace was clean and sober and had been for over a year. It was hard to believe, but Marisa clung to that promise.

"There he is." The jubilation in her brother's voice was almost unbearable.

Marisa's chest tightened with emotion. She wanted Chance to enjoy life again, but she wanted him to be safe too.

Chance whirled the chair and rolled toward the doorway to watch for Ace. When had her brother last been this eager and happy? He'd been the one who refused to see old friends. He'd refused outings to his former team's ballgames and made her promise not to tell a soul he was in town. And she'd let him huddle away in this lonely room, depressed and hopeless in the name of safety.

Then Ace had stormed the gates with the sheer force of his personality and refused to take no for an answer.

Guilt suffused her. Was she, as Ace accused, holding her brother back?

She finished repacking the tote as the lean cowboy appeared in the doorway. He towered over Chance and looked cowboy-sexy in faded old jeans and a gray plaid button-down opened over a black T-shirt.

"Ready?"

His grin matched her brother's. She wished she could be as confident that all would be well.

"Stoked," Chance answered. "Let's do this."

He and Chance exchanged fist bumps.

Stoked? How about petrified?

Ace caught her expression, and his grin softened to a smile. Her stomach fluttered. In spite of her reservations, she smiled back.

"Hey." He stepped around her brother's chair and approached her. In a quiet baritone, he said, "Get the worry out of your eyes. This is supposed to be fun. We'll fish the upper pond near the house and maybe take the boat out on the lake if he wants to. Afterward, the gang's coming over for dinner. Nothing crazy or dangerous. They're eager to see you and show off their new families."

"We can't stay that long." She hoisted the tote bag.

Ace took it from her. "Sure you can. Relax. That's what a day off is for."

They started down the hall. One of the other nurse aides stepped out of a resident's room and patted a hand over her heart. Another joined her fingers together in a heart shape.

Marisa's lips quivered. They had started to tease her about the hot cowboy, and regardless of how many times she'd explained that there was nothing between them, the silliness continued.

She was acutely aware of the effect Ace had on the rest of the staff and a good many of the older ladies in the home.

Chance shot ahead, beating them to the door in his eagerness.

Ace held the door for her brother and then touched her back as she walked through. It was only a polite gesture, but an unwanted thrill shimmied across her nerve endings.

Ace pointed a key fob at a white van parked beside the curb. Locks clicked and the side door slid open. He clicked again and a lift ramp descended.

Marisa stared in surprise. "Where did you get this?"

"Borrowed from a friend. We could manage in a regular vehicle, but I thought this would be easier for today."

"Won't your friend need it?"

"The van is for his wife, and she's is in the hospital, so he's driving my truck. Fair trade."

Ace didn't have to do this. He could be anywhere he wanted to be instead of here with a paralyzed man and his reluctant, ungrateful sister. But he'd gone to all this trouble to make things easier for Chance and to save him the indignity of being lifted like a child.

A man like that could do funny things to a woman's resistance.

Ace moved close to her brother, supportive and watchful, as Chance drove up on the ramp. In seconds, the chair and man were safely inside the van. Ace shut the door with a metallic click. Chance grinned at them through the window.

The ice around her heart melted a little more.

She walked to the passenger door, fighting emotion. She was grateful. Really she was. But a spiffy, handicap-accessible van didn't erase her misgivings.

Still, Ace had done this with no motive except to give Chance an outing.

She was having a hard time with that.

Ace reached around and grabbed the handle before she could open her door. She turned, placed a hand on his upper arm. It was rock hard with muscle. A lesser woman would swoon a little. Or at least, salivate. And maybe she was a lesser woman.

"Thank you. The van is very thoughtful."

They were mere inches apart, her back against the sun-warmed vehicle, his arm almost around her as he held to the handle. She smelled his aftershave, a woodsy, outdoor blend that suited him well. His shirt sleeve grazed her ear, tickling.

How easy it would be to step closer and be in his arms. She didn't, of course. They were both here for Chance, not for each other. And that's the way she wanted it to stay. The lesson she'd learned had been too hard and painful to take the risk.

The cowboy studied her for several seconds, solemn and thoughtful while her insides tumbled.

"My pleasure."

And she believed him.

Then he winked, popped the door open and waited politely while she climbed inside.

Chance was jabbering something, but the roar in her head drowned him out.

She still had feelings for Ace Caldwell, and that could not be a good thing.

ACE LEFT Marisa and Chance in the living room at the Triple C with Connie and two glasses of fresh iced tea and excused himself. He trotted upstairs to his bedroom, far from his company, to make the phone call.

He hadn't talked to his sponsor in four months. He was a sponsor himself these days. He shouldn't need this. He could have talked to Nate, but his brother couldn't understand the way another alcoholic could.

It had taken him too long to think of himself in those terms. An alcoholic, a man with a real problem that required outside assistance to overcome. Chance, who wasn't to blame for his problems, *deserved* help. Ace wasn't so sure he deserved anything, but neither of them could get free by himself. The truth hurt, but it would also, as the Bible reminded him, set him free.

Once inside his bedroom, he closed the door and took a seat on the end of the chaise lounge. The leather gave with his weight, and the deep gray color reminded him of Marisa's eyes.

She was scared. Of him. Of today. Of what other disaster he'd bring upon her and her brother.

Another painful truth.

"God, let today be the start of something better for Marisa and Chance. Show me how to do my part."

He continued praying, though now in his head, as he tapped in the numbers and spoke to Chet, an AA pal who'd been sober for thirteen years. Ace looked forward to the day he could make that claim.

"I'm going fishing," he said.

"Should be fun. What's the problem?"

Ace emitted a sigh. "The cooler of beer I want to take along."

"I hear you. What are you going to do?"

"Well." He laughed softly. "I'm not taking that cooler."

"Good plan." Chet's gravelly voice told of too many cigarettes and late nights singing in smoky honky-tonks. The man could pick a mean guitar. "So what else is bothering you?"

Marisa. The woman I used to love. "There's this girl along, with her brother. The one I told you about."

"The girl you're in love with."

"Was. And the brother who was injured in the wreck."

"Ah, the guilt. Wishing you could drown the accusing voices."

"Something like that."

"Why are you with them? Wallowing? Or making amends?"

Ace leaned forward, his forearms on his thighs, and stared at the geometric pattern in the blue-and-gray carpet, seeing nothing except the faces of Marisa and Chance.

"Step nine, but I care about them, too. I want to make their lives easier, but Marisa is afraid of me and what I represent."

"The accident?"

"Yeah." He scratched an itchy spot behind his ear, more frustration than actual itch. "I want them in my life, and if I can help Chance find some balance in his, I'm going to do it."

"All well and good as long as you don't let the bad memories drag you backwards."

"I won't. Ever." Then he admitted his biggest worry. "But sometimes *ever* sounds too long."

"Been there. This isn't new ground for any alcoholic, but it's something you have to work through and conquer."

Ace's fingers tightened on the phone. "Have you conquered it?"

"I have, but I'm always mindful that it can sneak up on me again." Chet took a breath. "You know what's behind you, Ace. Grief, remorse, damaged relationships. Do you want any of that again? Is the booze worth it?"

"Not even close." Ace's grip eased and he leaned back,

the anxiety leaching from his neck and shoulders. "God's carried me this far, and I'm still hanging on to Him. Today I just needed to talk to someone I could hear audibly."

Chet chuckled softly. "I understand."

"I know you do. That's why I called."

The conversation continued while Ace spilled his guts in honest revelation and Chet offered encouragement and advice. His sponsor said the same things Ace would say to Don or anyone else fighting the demon, and the words calmed him.

Finally, the conversation lagged, and Ace said, "I'm good now, Chet. Sorry to keep you this long."

"No apology needed. You know that. I'm here, day or night."

"Right. And I appreciate it. My family is great—"

"But they don't get it."

"Exactly." He was the fly in the otherwise delicious Caldwell soup.

"Text me a picture of the big one you catch."

"Will do." Ace breathed easy, confident now of one more good day. "Thanks, Chet."

After they hung up, Ace slid the phone into his hip pocket and strode to his nightstand. Inside was a bottle of aspirin, courtesy of his boozing days, a Bible, the first sobriety coin he'd received at AA, and a bag of cinnamon disks. He ripped open the bag and popped a candy into this mouth.

Cinnamon was his addiction of choice these days.

He pocketed the one-month token, his reminder that he'd come a very long way.

He bounded down the staircase, energized and positive. As he rounded into the living room, Marisa turned her head. His chest got a funny hitch, and for a second, he couldn't breathe. She was so pretty, her dark hair lying straight against her shoulders beneath the pink cap. Her T-shirt was pink too, as were the strings in her athletic shoes. He'd forgotten how much she loved the color because all he'd seen her wear at the care center were regulation scrubs.

Pretty in pink and full of anxiety. He felt her tension clear across the room.

He rubbed his hands together as he rounded the couch and faced Chance. "Ready?"

"You bet." Eager energy flowed from the other man. This was the Chance of old. He unlocked his chair and maneuvered around the furniture to the entryway.

Marisa's movement was less enthusiastic, but she accepted the snack basket Connie carried from the kitchen. Ace grabbed the small cooler, remembering his conversation with his sponsor. From now on, a cooler meant soda and water, ice tea and lemonade, refreshment without the bitter aftertaste.

He'd parked the van below the tidy new ramp built by the men of the Triple C in one easy day. In minutes they were loaded up and headed toward the nearest pond.

Marisa sat in the passenger seat next to him, silent, her hands twisted in her lap. She'd said exactly nothing since he'd come down the stairs.

As he pulled off the beaten service road and bumped down the grassy slope to the pond, Chance leaned forward. "I caught a six-pounder here last time."

Ace's neck tensed. He cast a glance at Marisa. She

stared straight ahead, her face pale. He knew what she was thinking. The last time they'd been fishing together. When Chance could walk down this slope on his own two legs.

Ace tossed a reply over one shoulder. "You remember that?"

"Sure, I do. A man catches a bass that big and you make him toss it back?" Chance gave a pretend groan and slapped his chest. "Painful."

"Hey, I snapped a picture. You have evidence."

"True, and let me tell you, I showed it to all my players. They were impressed."

His players, the high school boys he used to coach in baseball and football. This was the first time Chance had mentioned anything about his life before the accident. Maybe he was making progress. Now, if they could convince Marisa of that, this might be a good day.

"Maybe you'll catch him again. Only now, he'll weigh seven or eight."

"That's the plan." Chance put a hand on Marisa's shoulder. She jumped. "What did I do with that picture? Do you remember?"

"I have it somewhere. I can look."

"No need. I'm going for bigger and better today. Get the camera ready."

Ace braked to a stop thirty yards from the pond bank, suddenly aware that he'd failed again. He leaned his arms on the steering wheel and stared at the rough terrain with no dock and no ramp. Why hadn't he thought of this?

Ten acres of gleaming water stretched before them, and Chance couldn't get down to the edge.

Marisa leaned toward the windshield, her mouth set in a tight line. "We can't get the wheelchair over that."

"Sure we can." Chance was not to be deterred. "It might be bumpy, but I'll manage."

Marisa whipped around to face her brother. "You can't."

Chance's words tightened. "Are you ever going to let me do anything?"

"I'm worried about you. Haven't you been hurt enough? I knew this trip was a terrible idea."

Ace stared at the arguing siblings. This was his fault. He should have thought through the logistics of bringing a wheelchair to a rugged ranch pond. Never mind that he'd remembered to brush hog around the edges. Chance had to get down there first.

"Stop arguing. We'll fix this." He slammed the van into gear, backed up the incline to the road and pointed the hood toward the ranch house.

Marisa crossed her arms and chewed on her bottom lip. It sure was a pretty lip, and he could think of better things to do with it than gnaw the skin off. And wasn't he ridiculous for thinking about kissing her when she'd rather see him tossed in the pond with a rock around his neck?

At the big supply barn, he tapped an app on his phone, and the giant overhead door lifted. He drove in, parked, and said, "Sit tight. Think good thoughts. I'll be right back."

In less time than it took to shake off the desire to be somewhere alone with Marisa, they were back at the pond. He tossed several wooden feed pallets on the ground between the van and the pond and set up a pair of thick two-by-six boards to serve as a ramp onto and off the pallets. It would be tricky and require his and Marisa's help—if she would cooperate.

Marisa got out of the van and adjusted one or two pallets, surprising him when she said, "This was a good idea, Ace."

"Think it will work?"

She studied it and then looked at Chance's chair, already parked on the lowered van ramp and ready to roll. "A little bumpy maybe, but it should be fine. What do you think, Chance?"

Chance's grin said it all. "Let's get this party started."

With Ace guiding on one side and Marisa on the other, Chance rumbled over the wooden pallets, onto the smooth grass and down to the edge of the pond. He locked his wheels into place with a happy flourish. "Perfect!"

Over his head, Marisa and Ace exchanged a smile, another surprise. He saw it then. She wasn't mad at him. She was scared. The truth bruised his heart. He didn't want her to be scared. He wanted her to be the happy woman she'd been before the accident.

"I'll get the bait and tackle."

He'd opened the back of the van when she appeared beside him, standing close enough that he caught a whiff of coconut. He used to tease her about washing her hair in coconut milk.

As he reached for his enormous tackle box, she reached for the rods and reels. Their shoulders bumped. They were leaning halfway inside the rear of the van, side by side. He swiveled to look at her. Her beautiful gray eyes widened, and a smile lifted the lips he'd never forgotten.

"He's ecstatic."

Ace touched her cheek. "Don't be worried. Be happy that he's happy."

She bit down on her lip and his gaze was drawn there again.

"I barely remember what that feels like."

Ace bracketed her face with both hands, the tackle box forgotten. "Then let me remind you."

Something in his chest jittered as he stared into her face and was awash with memories of the woman he'd once loved.

He was probably making a big mistake, but the tug inside him when he was close to Marisa was like the positive and negative poles of a magnet—irresistible.

Slowly, he drew her up until they were standing outside the van, closer than a whisper. A thousand thoughts darted through his head, too fast for him to hold on to except the one that wanted to be with Marisa and erase her worries. He didn't know why it mattered so desperately, but it did.

When she didn't slap him or step away, he pressed his mouth to hers, tasting the lemon from her tea and the warmth he'd never found in any other woman's kiss.

He realized it then. He was as scared as she was, but for different reasons. Taking exquisite care and with all the tenderness rising in his blood, he caressed the sides of her face and deepened the kiss.

A soft sigh emanated from her throat, and Ace thought

his knees might give away. She pressed closer, and when he would have taken the kiss up another notch, Chance's voice jarred him back to reality.

"Hey, you two, are we gonna fish or what?"

Still cupping Marisa's face, Ace placed one last soft kiss on her lips and whispered, "Or what."

A laugh gurgled up from her throat. Cheeks pink, she stepped away, gathered the fishing equipment, and headed toward her brother.

Ace removed his hat and scrubbed the top of his head, grinning.

Now, they were getting somewhere.

CHAPTER 9

*M*arisa kept her distance from Ace, but she was acutely aware of him. He fished from the bank fifty yards away near a willow tree weeping into the murky water. Chance fished where he'd parked the wheelchair, casting the reel with expert ease while she hovered in a folding lawn chair next to him, thinking too much.

She'd let Ace kiss her, and she'd liked it. If not for Chance, she'd probably still be behind that van or in it, kissing the cowboy who'd caused all her problems. Or at least, the most recent ones.

What in the world was the matter with her? Was she genetically predisposed toward men who were bad for her?

Yet, Ace hadn't seemed so bad since he'd come back into their lives.

Frustrated by the confusion, she grabbed a can of bug spray and spritzed Chance's ankles.

"You already did that."

"Oh." She spritzed her own ankles, aware she'd done that too.

Chance rotated the handle of the reel. The Browning, Ace's favorite, made a whirring noise as the line wiggled its way back to shore. "Why aren't you fishing?"

"I'd rather watch you."

"Watching someone fish is boring. Grab a rod. Ace brought extras."

"What if I catch the big one?"

"Ha! Fat chance."

"Okay, little brother, now you're on." She grabbed one of the rods and attached a lure, aware that the only other times in her life that she'd been fishing had been with Ace. He'd taught her which lures to use.

Chance spread both elbows out to the side as if to push her away. "Move down the bank a little. You're in my spot."

She gave his shoulder a friendly shove. "Picky, picky."

"And stop talking. You'll scare the fish." His scowl teased, but she knew how serious a fisherman could be.

She made a face and, in search of a shady spot, moved into the space between him and Ace. Her brother was almost his old self today, joking, giving her and Ace a hard time. She loved that.

Ace had done this. The cowboy had seen what she hadn't and had acted on it in spite of her protests. He'd always had trouble with the word no. For Chance's sake, at least for today, she was glad.

Someone had mowed around the pond recently, and she credited Ace for that, too. She shouldn't have been so hard on him about the ramp, or the lack thereof. Chance's disability was new ground for him, too.

The admission felt right. Maybe the forgiveness she'd worked on for over a year was starting to take effect.

Or was she making excuses because she had trouble resisting a certain cowboy?

The unanswerable question. But forgiveness couldn't be a bad thing. She'd settle for that and leave the other alone. For now.

With a flick of her wrist, she cast her line, heard the *plunk*, and watched the lure sink. The sun was hot today, and she was glad for the dappled shade of a mulberry tree and the blessing of sunscreen. Had she remembered to put some on Chance? It wouldn't do for his hospital-pale skin to get sunburned. She bit her lip and quickly reeled in the line, propped the rod beside the scrubby tree and jogged to the van.

Chance shot her a questioning glance and then turned his attention back to the water.

She hauled her tote bag from the van to his chair. "I forgot the sunscreen."

Chance rolled his head back and shook it at the white, puffy clouds. "I'm not going to melt, Marisa."

She ignored his protests and smoothed the cream over his arms. "A burn is the last thing you need."

He gripped her hand, stopping her ministrations. "I *need* to fish. Come on, sis, lighten up. Just for today. Please."

Stung, she spun away, dropped the tube of sunscreen into her bag and wiped the remainder from her fingers to her arms. She was trying to take care of him. Didn't he understand?

"I could use a Mountain Dew." His tone was conciliatory. Sweet Chance, ever the peacemaker.

Mollified, she got the drink, took a bottled water for herself, and went back to her fishing spot. As she once more cast the line, she also cast a glance at the movement upstream. Ace held up a fish.

"Nice one," she called. "What kind is it?"

"Bass. Maybe a three pounder."

"Want a picture?"

"Sure. Proof is good, especially with competition from your brother. He plays hardball."

She trotted to him, swatting gnats that seemed to love her bug spray. Grasshoppers whirred past like tiny, green jets.

Taking Ace's phone—one of those fancy, expensive ones—she snapped a photo of the grinning cowboy and his catch. Suddenly, Chance whooped, and they both looked his way. His line bent, he rapidly whirled the reel, lifting the pole every few turns.

"He's got a good one." Ace's voice came close to her ear. He'd released his own catch and moved up next to her, close enough that she felt his body heat. Her own body heated up. Maybe it was the June sun, but she feared it was Ace Caldwell.

"Good for him," Ace said. The words were soft and proud, as if Ace wanted her brother to win their fierce fishing competition.

She watched him watching her brother. Ace's eyes glittered with the excitement of Chance's battle with the big one. Aligned with his strong jaw, Marisa's gaze was naturally drawn to his mouth. That half-smiling, sensuous mouth that had kissed her with such expertise and exquisite care.

"I got him. I got him!" Chance's exuberant voice carried across the water. "Woo-hoo!"

This was Chance's moment. Marisa tore her attention from the dangerous cowboy.

Holding the fish by the mouth, her brother lofted his catch. "Beat that, Ace of spades."

Ace raised both hands out to the side. "Is that the best you got? A minnow?"

Both men hooted.

She bumped the cowboy with her elbow. "He will definitely want a picture of that one."

"To my great despair." Ace emitted a fake groan and grabbed her hand. "Let's go weigh that monster. He caught a good one, but don't tell him I said so."

She snickered. "You'll never hear the end of it unless you catch one bigger."

"Don't I know it?" But his grin said he was delighted for her brother, and the light feeling moved over her again.

After the fish was weighed, measured, the obligatory photo taken and the fish tossed back into the water she said, "Anybody ready for a snack yet?"

"You bet. Let's see what Connie packed. I'll grab the basket." To Marisa, Ace said, "Help me carry the drinks?"

"Sure."

"You two kids go ahead." Chance waved them away,

energy and pleasure coming off him in waves. "Another big one is calling my name."

Marisa looked at Ace and lifted her shoulders in an amused shrug. "I think he's having fun."

"What about you?" Ace's expression was serious, searching, as if her opinion mattered.

She pondered for a moment. Pondered him, the question, her tangled feelings. "I am. Thanks to you."

That simple admission brought a light to Ace's green eyes. He offered a palm, questioning. She joined her hand to his. Why not? Holding hands wasn't a commitment, and the ground between the pond and the van was uneven.

Admit it, Marisa, you want to be close to him, and the rocky terrain has nothing to do with it.

His skin was rough with calluses she found masculine and alluring, and his grip was firm and strong, a reminder that he was a man and she was a woman. She'd always appreciated the differences, especially with Ace.

She recalled earlier when he'd cupped her face with those cowboy-tough hands, recalled the thrill his tender touch had sent through her body like shock-waves.

She wasn't over him. The question was, what was she going to do about it? For months, her focus on Chance's health and her anger had blocked all other thought and emotion. Being with Ace again was like thawing cold feet —it hurt, but it felt good too.

Hand in hand, they returned to the van, the questions lingering in her thoughts right next to the kiss. Was she crazy to want it to happen again?

Marisa slid a glance toward Ace. He caught her

looking and smiled. Not a cocky grin. A gentle smile that sent her mind reeling and her blood rushing.

Neither of them spoke, but the air became super charged, like the moment before a lighting strike.

It was there. It was always going to be there. Time and tragedy hadn't erased the love she felt for this man.

They stepped to the back of the opened van, the doors blocking them from sight. She was intensely aware of that fact. Chance couldn't see them. If Ace kissed her again, or if she kissed him, Chance wouldn't know and tease her. Or ask questions she couldn't answer.

"Marisa." Ace broke the silence, but then he looked lost, as if, like her, he didn't know where to go from this point. He raised her hand to his chest and merely stood there, holding her with his eyes. She read the questions and the hurt. Strange to realize he'd been hurt in all this too.

"I'm not mad at you anymore." She wanted to be, but she couldn't muster the strength. Not with him six inches away. Not after today when he'd given her back her brother, at least in part. Especially since she'd fought against making the trip. And she'd been wrong.

His chest rose, and he exhaled, long and slow. "I'm glad. It kills me to know I hurt you."

He reeled her in and held her, quiet and easy. She settled against his body, where she'd always fit so perfectly, sliding her arms around his neck, head tilted back to look into his handsome face. Their eyes met and held, the electric pull between them undeniable.

Marisa tiptoed up to meet him, lips parted, wanting to

kiss him more than anything she could think of at the moment.

Ace was never one to resist such an invitation. When his lips touched hers, Marisa sighed into him.

Nobody had ever kissed her the way Ace could, as if she were the most treasured woman on the planet. As if he meant it.

Grass tickled her ankles and a grasshopper landed in her hair, but the fog in her brain was too pleasant to do more than notice.

When they finally stopped kissing—a tragedy, she thought—Ace continued to hold her and rocked from side to side. She put her ear against his chest, heard the thunder, and preened a little to know she'd caused the galloping heartbeat.

After a bit, he murmured against her hair. By now, the grasshopper had given up and moved on. "What were we supposed to be doing back here?"

Marisa snickered. "Snacks and drink, maybe? I'm not sure."

"I hope Chance isn't starving."

The mention of her brother jolted Marisa. She jerked away. Ace's arms fell to his sides, and she wanted to be back in them, held close as if the world was right.

"I totally forgot." She slapped a hand over her mouth. How could she forget about her brother, the most important person in her life?

Stupid, stupid. Like before.

Ace reached for her again. "Marisa. Wait."

She turned aside, frantically searching for balance in a world gone crazy.

Before she could grab the picnic basket and head back to the pond, she heard the rattle of wheelchair against wood.

Her heart stopped. He couldn't be. Not that.

Chance called out. "Whatever you two are doing, stop now. I'm heading your way."

"No!" Marisa flung a wild look at Ace and bolted from behind the doors. "Chance, no."

But she was too late. Chance wheeled toward her, across the bumpy pallets with no support on either side to keep the wheels aligned.

Ace passed her, moving in a lope toward her brother. "Chance. Wait."

The words came too late. The chair's left wheel slipped off one edge. And then, disaster. As if in slow motion, the wheelchair tilted to the left, and Chance tumbled down, the chair coming to rest on top of him. Rubber wheels spun in the air.

Marisa heard a cry, her own, as she rushed to her brother's aid. Ace was there first, kneeling on the ground next to an upturned Chance.

"Are you okay?"

Marisa was wild. "No, he's not okay. He's hurt. Look." She pointed at Chance's cheek. "He's bleeding."

In a shaky voice, Chance said, "Only a scratch. I'm all right."

"You can't possibly know that. You could have a broken leg!"

Chance's expression went flat. "Wouldn't matter much, would it?"

"Let's get you up." Ace, muscles flexing, grasped the chair. "Marisa, balance Chance. I'll take the weight."

As quickly as he'd tumbled, Chance was upright again. But it didn't matter. He was hurt. Her fears had proved correct. Ace had gotten him into another disaster. And once again, she'd been complicit.

While Chance had been heading toward disaster, she'd been reveling in Ace's arms.

What kind of sister would do such a thing?

She flew around like a hummingbird on steroids, dabbing blood from Chance's cheek, chin, and left elbow, checking and rechecking him for injuries.

Ace quietly made an ice pack and held it against Chance's scraped and swollen cheek.

"Stupid of me to try that." Chance sat slumped while they cared for him. The joy had disappeared. Darkness settled over him again.

"It's my fault. We never should have come. I knew it was too dangerous." She gazed at Ace, tall and solemn at her brother's side. She'd been kissing him. *Kissing him!* While her brother suffered the consequences. "We need to go home."

Chance's grip on her wrist stilled her efforts. "No."

"But you're hurt."

"I've had worse, and you know it." His eyes begged her, and she was weak. Hadn't she proved as much today?

"Let's get you back to the ranch house," Ace said. "We can decide there."

THE RIDE back to the house proved tense. Chance tried to

convince his sister he was all right while Marisa looked as though the world had ended.

Ace mulled the incident, trying to decide if he was guilty of anything, though he knew he wasn't. Chance needed to be a man. Everyone had mishaps. Ace refused to believe today was a mistake, but he regretted the distance now apparent between him and Marisa. They'd made such great progress today. For a while, they'd been back to normal.

He shot a glance her way. She sat hunched in the passenger's seat, her hands tight in her lap, knuckles white. He hated seeing her upset. If he thought she'd let him, he'd stop the van and hold her until the shakes disappeared and she liked him again. He needed for her to be all right.

When they reached the main house, Chance let Marisa wheel him up the ramp, something he'd refused a couple of hours ago. The fall was a setback, no doubt about it.

Marisa would hate him again, blame him. If it made her feel better, he'd let her.

Inside the house, Connie sized up the incident with her usual expediency and sent Marisa to the kitchen for a round of ice tea.

"But, Chance needs m—"

"Marisa, I'm fine." Chance blew out a heavy breath. "Stop it."

Connie patted her arm, gentle but insistent. "You are a good sister, *querida*, so devoted, but this has been traumatic for you, too. Believe me, I am good at this. Three wild boys I raised, always getting bumps and bruises. I will tell you about them sometime. Go, now. Your brother needs something cold to drink."

Marisa cast a final, worried look at Chance and headed toward the kitchen.

Ace held back a grin. Connie could command an army if she wanted to. Over Chance's head, she hitched her chin toward the kitchen, indicating for him to follow Marisa.

Smart and intuitive, Connie was giving him an opportunity to talk to Marisa alone.

"Thanks," he mouthed.

He found Marisa standing in front of an open cabinet, staring at a row of shiny dishes. She'd stopped shaking, and for that he was grateful.

He walked up beside her, reached over her head and took down four glasses. Without a word, avoiding his questioning gaze, she accepted them one at a time and filled them with ice from the spout in the refrigerator door.

Ace leaned his backside against the counter, watching her, wanting to say the right thing and having no idea what that was.

"Don't go." *That* was a winning conversation starter if he'd ever heard one. He shifted his weight to one hip, wanting to touch her and knowing she didn't want that now. But she had.

One step forward and another back, like some kind of crazy, futile waltz.

"Chance needs to be checked over by the nurse." Marisa stood between him and the stainless steel fridge, holding two clear glasses of ice. "Maybe I should take him to the emergency room."

In the big, rock-tile and birch-wood kitchen, she looked small and needy. Uncertain, too, and scared. Every instinct Ace possessed told him to protect her from the world and all its trouble. The tragedy lay in that he was responsible for so much of it.

"He's okay," Ace said. "Embarrassed, but not injured. But if it'll make you feel better, I'll take him into town to the ER."

She sucked in a long breath and set the glasses on the counter. "He'd be furious."

"Then stay. Connie's cooking a feast for dinner. The family will be here. They want to see you, Marisa." He wanted her here, and if laying on a little guilt did the trick, he wasn't above it. "Nate and Gilbert built the ramp so Chance could come. Connie has brisket and ribs in the smoker. She knows barbecue is your favorite."

"All that trouble. For us."

It hurt him to know she'd rarely been fussed over in her life. If she'd let him, he'd do a lot of fussing. So would his family.

But today, after the incident, she'd pulled away again, an island alone, close enough to see but too far away to touch.

A throb started in his chest.

Marisa turned her back to take out a pitcher of tea, and he thought she'd refuse the invitation. She came back to the counter, filled the glasses, set the pitcher aside with a *tink* of glass against tile, and glanced toward the living room before finally agreeing. "Okay."

And though she stayed, she said little and kept her distance from him, the man she'd kissed with passion hours before.

The day had lost its joy, and Ace knew he'd failed again.

CHAPTER 10

ce stretched out on the chaise lounge, bare feet crossed at the ankles, pondering the day's events. He'd done little else since Chance's fall. Was this his fault? Should he have thought about a portable ramp for use at the pond? Maybe. Probably.

Even though Chance was a grown man, Ace had promised Marisa that nothing would happen. And it had.

At his side, a bag of cinnamon candy lay open. He had one candy in his mouth and one at the ready. This was definitely a double cinnamon night. Maybe a cup of chamomile too.

Connie had tried to talk to him when he'd returned from taking the Foreman duo home, but he hadn't been in the mood.

If ever he should want a drink, it was now, but strangely, he didn't. He wanted Chance to be healthy. He wanted Marisa to forgive him. Maybe he wanted more than that from her, but it wasn't only what *he* wanted. It was about her happiness. About making her life easier and better. Marisa deserved so much more than she'd ever gotten.

His cell phone lay on his chest atop the white-and-orange Oklahoma State T-shirt he'd thrown on over a pair of boxers after a long, contemplative shower. He did some of his best thinking under a warm spray of water.

He rolled the candy with his tongue and glanced at the clock. Not that late.

She probably didn't want to hear from him.

He tapped the icon of her smiling face anyway. He'd taken the photo at the care center weeks ago. She'd been laughing with Chance at some silly YouTube video and had cringed when he'd unexpectedly snapped the picture. Ace had looked at it a thousand times. She was so pretty with those soft gray eyes and that clear, smooth skin, her dark hair swept back from her face and shiny pink studs in her ears.

He listened to the phone's *brrr,* surprisingly nervous, but every bit as compelled to hear Marisa's voice and assure himself that she was all right.

She didn't pick up for the longest time, and he suspected she was ignoring him. Caller ID had its drawbacks. He let it ring anyway.

Breathless, her voice came over the line. A thrill tingled the skin on his arms.

"Are you speaking to me?" he asked softly.

"Apparently."

His heart thundered. He didn't know if she was joking or serious. "You okay?"

"I wasn't the injured party."

Yes, you were. In so many ways, I hurt you. Maybe not today, but I hurt you. God forgive me.

"Chance?" he asked.

"As soon as he got settled in bed, the charge nurse checked him over thoroughly. No serious injuries. He thinks I overreacted."

Ace let out a breath he didn't know he'd been holding. Her reaction *had* been over the top. He'd watched Chance fall. The short, quick tumble hadn't been serious enough to do anything more than bump and scrape, but the medical confirmation relieved Marisa. He could hear it in her voice.

"You were upset."

"Terrified."

"Understandable."

A tick of silence and then that soft, smooth-as-butter voice. "When did you become so understanding?"

"After I needed a lot of it for myself."

"Oh."

In that one little breathy word, he heard her contemplation. She'd never asked about the dark journey he'd been on. She'd been on one of her own at the same time, though hers hadn't been her fault.

Pulse ticking against his collarbone like a tiny hammer of uncertainty, he said, "I had fun today until the accident. Did you?"

A hesitation, and then Marisa's murmur tickled his ear. And maybe his ego. "Yes."

Hope sprang up. She really didn't hate him. She might want to, but she didn't. "We could do it again."

"I don't think so."

"If not here at the ranch, somewhere else. Anywhere you want to go."

"For Chance?"

No. A date. You and me. But he didn't say that. She'd hang up on him if he did.

"Whatever you want it to be."

"I'll think about it."

The waltz moved forward again. Progress. He'd take it. "I'm not sorry I kissed you. It was…beautiful."

That silenced her for a few seconds. He could hear her soft breathing and wished he was with her in the flesh. He'd kiss her again.

"Chance wouldn't have fallen if—"

He could practically see her biting her lip.

"Ifs are futile, Marisa. I learned that the hard way. You can't undo what's been done." He could only move forward and pray for forgiveness and not to mess up any more.

She went silent again, the truck wreck a ghost between them waiting to jump out and send them both scurrying to their safe places.

He wanted to be her safe place, to protect her and give her all the things she'd never had. Ace rubbed a palm down the front of his shirt, over the orange letters that covered his heart. He owed her big time. Chance too. But something else stirred, down deep where he couldn't see yet.

"I should go," she murmured.

Ace uncrossed his ankles and sat up. He'd lost her. "Tired?"

"A little."

"Tomorrow, then?"

Her quiet chuckle came through the line. "Can I stop you?"

His mood buoyed. She'd laughed. Maybe he hadn't lost her after all.

"No. I'll be there."

"Tomorrow then." And the line went dead.

MONDAY'S ALARM clock seemed to ring earlier than on any other day of the week.

Marisa fumbled for the *silence* button atop the device and dragged herself upright, the comforter falling to her waist. She wouldn't be so tired if she'd gone to sleep after the phone call from Ace. The trouble was, she hadn't. A slideshow of the outing, of Ace, of kissing him, of Chance's fall and subsequent injuries, played in her head over and over again.

Groggy, she shoved her hair back and stumbled to the bathroom for a face splash and to dress for the day.

Chance said she'd overreacted. Had she? She'd certainly overreacted to Ace, but try as she might, and Lord knew she'd tried, she couldn't regret their improved relationship. Hating him had worn her out. Granted, the truce was shaky, but it was still a relief.

The kissing? Well, that was something totally different to consider.

And consider Marisa did as she readied for her shift at the daycare center in stretchy capris and a loose blue top. Ace always commented when she wore blue. Not that she would see him before tonight or that she even cared what he thought.

Yes, you do.

With a groan, she smoothed a hand over the gauzy shirt and, after grabbing an apple from the kitchen, headed to work.

A hint of sunrise teased the horizon when she pulled into the parking space. Gray shadows still shrouded the landscape, visible but vague. Janey's SUV was already here, and the lights were on inside Kids' Care, as usual, though they had five minutes to spare before the doors officially opened at six.

Three cars pulled into the lot behind her. The day had begun for some parents and their children. Getting up and ready this early was hard for her. She couldn't imagine the challenge of adding a child to the morning rush. But she wouldn't mind trying if life hadn't thrown Chance such a terrible curveball. Now, she tried not to the think of the family she'd always longed for but had only experienced vicariously.

Inside the daycare, Janey came out of her office and greeted her with a tight nod before unlocking the front doors. Marisa frowned at her boss's back. Janey was normally a cheerful, energetic morning person. Was something wrong?

When she heard Janey's boisterous laugh at something one of the parents said, Marisa shook off the odd sense of foreboding, clocked in and went to her classroom to set up for the day. Only little Mattie arrived this early, and the toddler would sleep until the rest of the children arrived.

Clare stumbled through the classroom door toting a giant travel mug, blurry eyed, her red hair in a messy bun.

"Rough weekend?"

Clare moaned. "You don't even want to know." She plunked her cup on a shelf. "But I'll tell you anyway."

Marisa chuckled. "How did I know you'd say that?"

"Paul and I went to a pool party last night that lasted way too late. We played water polo, among other crazy, muscle destroying games, chased each other with giant water guns, played volleyball, and didn't crawl home until after one."

Marisa fought a pinch of envy. "Sounds fun."

"Every muscle in my body hurts."

"That part doesn't sound so fun."

The redhead laughed. "It was worth it. Paul is now convinced we need to save up for one of those above-ground pools. They're not *that* expensive."

They were to Marisa, though she'd wondered if water therapy would be beneficial to Chance. If she could afford a pool for Chance...but she couldn't. "I hope you get one. Both of you work hard. You need to kick back and have fun when you can."

"So do you." Clare sipped from her cup, put it aside and began gathering items for today's lesson plan on texture and touch. "But you never go anywhere."

"Sure I do. I went fishing yesterday."

The other teacher narrowed her eyes. "Fishing? With who?"

Marisa pulled a plastic box from a shelf and took out a set of finger puppets for circle time. "My brother."

"Oh." Clare's shoulders dropped in mock despair. "I was hoping some hottie had finally caught your eye."

Marisa turned her attention to filling sippy cups with milk for breakfast.

Clare came around in front of her. "You got too quiet too fast. Was there anybody else along besides your brother?"

She snapped a lid onto a pink cup. "Nobody important."

"Then why are you blushing?"

"I'm not." But she touched her warm cheeks anyway.

"Come on. Spill it. Who is he and where have you been hiding him?"

"He's...a friend. The fishing trip was something he wanted to do for Chance, and they allowed me to tag along. That's all."

"How good of a friend? I've never seen you blush before. He's got to be pretty special." Clare got the ABC place mats from the cupboard.

"Long story."

"We have all day."

Marisa laughed in spite of her discomfort. "Ace and I dated in the past, and that's all I'm going to say about him."

"But—"

With a head shake, Marisa saluted her friend with the last sippy cup and went to the doorway to greet the first parent of the day. Some things couldn't be discussed. Not yet. Not until she figured out what to do about Ace Caldwell.

THE FIRST TWO hours passed in the usual business of settling toddlers in for the day, getting them fed, toileted, and into free play.

Marisa was sitting on the mat rolling a ball back and forth to two little boys when Janey stepped into the classroom.

"Marisa, could you come into my office for a minute, please?"

Marisa's stomach lurched. The boss didn't look happy.

"Okay." She directed the two boys to roll the ball to one another and followed an unusually silent Janey down the short hall. Tension tightened Marisa's shoulders. Something was wrong. She could feel it.

The inside of Janey's office was like the woman, cheerful and kid-oriented. Photos of her grown children with her grandchildren lined her desk. Four kids and seven grandkids. Like Marisa, Janey adored children.

The boss motioned toward one of a pair of blue padded chairs. "Sit down, Marisa. We need to talk."

Janey lacked her usual smile.

Growing more anxious by the second, Marisa lowered herself to the seat. She gripped the chair arms. "Have I done something wrong?"

"Not at all." A distressed frown wrinkled Janey's forehead. "The children and parents love you, and you've been a great employee."

Marisa's pulse jumped, pounded.

She'd *been* a great employee?

"I appreciate that. I love teaching kids, and this job means a lot to me."

"I know, I know." Janey drew in a deep breath and

sighed, the sound heavy and troubled. "That's what makes this so difficult."

Marisa went from foreboding to full blown terror. She was afraid to speak, afraid to ask. She stared at her boss, hoping her fears were unsubstantiated.

They weren't.

"I'm so sorry, Marisa. Believe me, if there was a way to avoid this, I would, but with the new daycare taking so many of our kids, we don't need you anymore."

"But my class has lost only one child. Clare can't handle all our students alone."

"Currently, the one-year-old class has three teachers and now only needs two. I'm moving Veronica into your position. She's been here more than a year."

And Marisa had been here less than half that.

"I see."

"Please understand, you aren't being fired. This is a layoff. I'd keep you on if I could. I wrestled with the books all weekend trying to come up with another solution. You were meant to work with children. I mean that. But I can't afford any extras right now."

Marisa nodded, numb. All the compliments in the world wouldn't pay the bills. "When is my last day?"

Let it be the end of the month. Give me time to job hunt and juggle the bills again.

"I'm afraid it's today. Veronica will take over after lunch." Janey stood. "I'll be glad to give you a glowing reference."

Somehow Marisa managed a "thank you" and left the office.

No matter what Janey called it, the result was the same. She'd been fired.

AFTER A LONG DAY of loading feeder cattle into eighteen-wheelers bound for Kansas, Ace hit the showers before the drive to Clay City.

Yesterday had been shaky, but he and Marisa had ended on a good note. He'd wanted to call or text her all day, but he'd been too busy and figured she was too.

He was anxious to see her again.

As he aimed his truck toward the highway, he pondered his happy mood. He should be dead tired, but energy flowed through every cell. Energy generated by Marisa.

And Chance, of course, though somewhere along the way, his desire to bring Chance out of his shell had expanded to include a renewed relationship with Marisa.

He gnawed at a cinnamon disk and pondered this pleasant revelation.

Had he progressed far enough in his recovery to start something new with a woman?

Yeah, he thought he had. A Clay City AA meeting was scheduled for later tonight, so he'd make his visit with Chance short enough to attend. Some of the other men had walked this road before him. He'd talk to them and get their take, but he thought he was good to go.

Once he arrived in Clay City, he made a stop at Walmart before heading into Sunset Manor with a package beneath his arm.

Chance was in his wheelchair, perusing the iPad Ace

had left for him. When Ace entered the room, he glanced up, one very bruised and puffy eye barely a slit.

"Whoa, Pal. What a shiner!"

The red scrape started on Chance's cheekbone and extended up over one eye and onto his forehead. When he grinned, his eye completely disappeared.

"I told the nurses I was breaking up a fight. Two women vying for my attention." Chance pumped his eyebrows. "Back me up, will you? They think I'm a rock star or something."

Ace bounced a fist against his chest. "I saw the whole thing. Gorgeous, both of them. Is the eye the worst of it?"

Chance held up his arm, bent at the elbow. A white bandage extended from wrist to elbow. "When I went down, my arm hit first, sheared the edge of the pallet and left behind some skin. Marisa insisted on this dressing, but it's only a scrape."

"She was scared."

"I know." Chance's cheerful mood dampened. "I shouldn't have tried such a dumb stunt. If I'd stayed right here in this room like she wanted me to, this wouldn't have happened."

"You hate this place."

"I might as well get used to it."

They weren't going back to square one if Ace could help it. "So what're you saying?"

"I'm saying I should listen to my sister and stay safely where no one has to pick me up off the ground like a helpless baby."

"Bull feathers. That's not your style." Ace dragged a straight-backed chair he'd commandeered from the nurses up close to Chance's side. "I've attended a lot of the ballgames you coached. What did you always say to your players when they lost the first game of a tournament?"

Chance narrowed his good eye in contemplation. Ace could see the wheels turning and the lotto numbers falling into place.

Slowly, Chance nodded and the familiar phrases rolled off his tongue. "Shake it off. You know your opponent now. Come back stronger next time."

Ace pointed an index finger. "There you go then. You had a fall. Got a little bruised but survived and learned. Now, shake it off and come back stronger."

The young man huffed. "This isn't baseball."

"No, but I've learned a lot of things in AA, and one of them is this: The game of life will beat you if you let it. That's the key. *If you let it.* You don't have to let it happen." He whipped the rolled poster from beneath his arm. "Brought you something."

Chance eyed the giant piece of paper. "What is that?"

"Be patient, coach. You're about to gloat." Choosing the spot most visible from anywhere in the room, especially the bed, Ace swaggered to the wall parallel to Chance's footboard. "Marisa won't mind if I move this."

"You'll be doing me a favor, but don't tell her I said that. If I have to look at those smiling kitty cats one more day, I'll cry."

"True. She could have chosen something manly cool like this." With a flourish, Ace smoothed the poster against the wall and, using the handful of thumb tacks in his shirt pocket, secured each corner. "Get a load of that bad boy."

He stepped to the side, his hopeful gaze on Chance.

A smile, distorted by the black eye but wide enough to crack his jaw, spread across the younger man's face. His eyes glowed. He leaned forward in his chair, and then finally rolled closer to stare at the giant version of himself and the massive bass he'd caught yesterday. The smile on his face then was the same as it was now. Minus a little distortion from the black eye.

"That's awesome, Ace. How did you do this?"

Ace's chest swelled like a hot air balloon. "The wonders of digital print and one hour photo. You like it?"

Tipped back in his chair, expression cocky, Chance tapped his chest. "Bragging rights are mine for a long time."

"Not if I can get you back out on that pond."

The cocky look dissipated. "I don't know, Ace."

"What do you mean, you don't know?" Ace moved in front of Chance's chair and stacked his fists on his hips. "I demand a rematch. You can't take a man down without giving him a chance to redeem himself."

Some of Chance's spark returned. He straightened slightly and eyed the poster. "I did beat the socks off you, didn't I? All you caught was a wimpy couple of pounds."

"Don't rub in it."

Once again, the slow grin moved over Chance's bruised face. "Why not? You would."

Relief eased through Ace. They were back on teasing ground, the dark mood gone. The poster had been genius, but Ace refused to take credit for it. He'd prayed. The idea had come.

"You're right. I would." He tapped a knuckle against the poster. "My rod and reel, so you owe me a rematch."

Chance blew out a derisive huff. "I'll just catch him again, or a bigger one. You won't stand a chance."

"Prove it, buddy. Put your money where your mouth is. Next Sunday afternoon. You. Me. The big bass."

Chance punched a fist against his palm. "Prepare for defeat. You're on."

Marisa chose that moment to breeze into the room, and Ace decided this was a good time to keep quiet. They'd break the news about another trip to the ranch after she'd had time to recover from yesterday's scare. Chance, apparently, had the same thought because he avoided her eyes.

And speaking of eyes, hers appeared red and swollen. Ace stepped toward her. "What's wrong? Have you been crying?"

She was tough. She never cried.

"Allergies." Avoiding his intense scrutiny, she dipped her head and fluttered around Chance without her usual false cheer. She checked his bandage, asked if he needed anything, and started to the door. She hadn't even hugged her brother.

Something was off. Way off. He'd never known Marisa to have "allergies."

"Marisa?"

She paused but didn't turn around. "We're busy on the floor. I can't stay and play."

The tone was terse, not at all the sweet voice he'd loved hearing last night. The voice that had given him this crazy hope.

"Can we talk later?"

"Not tonight. I'm really tired." She hurried out of the room.

The two men exchanged glances and then stared in bewilderment at the doorway.

"She never even mentioned my awesome poster," Chance said. "Wonder what's going on?"

"She said she was tired."

"You think that's all?"

Not wanting to worry his friend, Ace nodded. "Sure."

But she was always tired, so he didn't think that was the whole story.

His heart, energized moments ago, slowly descended, an elevator going down, down. Was it the fiasco at the pond and Chance's injuries, however slight? Or was it him? He knew she'd felt guilty for being with him when Chance fell. Did she regret last night's warm, almost tender conversation?

Had Marisa decided to despise him yet again?

CHAPTER 11

*M*arisa was right, Ace thought. He had a real hard time with rejection.

The next afternoon, Ace sat in the ranch office entering data into his computer, but his mind kept straying to last night at the care center.

Marisa had come in and out of her brother's room several times before Ace had left for his AA meeting, but she hadn't stayed long. He'd tried giving her a call after her shift ended, but she hadn't answered. So, he'd texted her a couple of times, and again, heard nothing.

Okay, maybe she *was* exhausted. The ranch trip, meant as a refresher, must have taken too much out of her.

Or she'd decided to freeze him out again to protect her brother from any more accidents.

He leaned back in his office chair and stared blankly at the screen.

Fear, his pals in AA had reminded him, was a powerful motivator. Marisa had operated on fear, exhaustion and hyper-responsibility too long. Ace wished he could do something about it.

He typed a few more entries, checked his stocks, and pushed up from the desk. Might as well knock off for the day. His mind wouldn't stop thinking about Marisa.

He shot a text to Nate and Gilbert. "If you don't need my help, I'm heading to Clay City."

Gilbert's reply was instant. "Go. We're finishing up with the hay meadow now."

Nate's text was more personal. "You've got it bad."

Ace shot back a distorted smiley face, pocketed the phone and headed for his truck. He hadn't been pulling his weight around the ranch, and he knew it. The rest of the family said they understood. He was glad someone did. He sure didn't.

Right now, all he could think of was finding out why Marisa had suddenly put him on the naughty list again.

He'd never visited her other job, but the PI had given him the address of Kids' Care Playschool, and he found it easily.

The problem was, he didn't see her car in the parking lot.

Now, he was really worried. Had she been coming down with the flu or something catastrophic like the Zika virus? And if she was sick, who was with her? She took care of Chance, little kids, the seniors, and everyone else, but who would take care of her?

He parked and went to the door. This one, too, had a security code box. Marisa and the children she loved were safe here. He, on the other hand, was stuck outside. So he pecked on the glass until a stout blonde with short hair and a kind expression opened it a crack.

"May I help you?"

Ace removed his hat and offered his most charming smile. "I'm Ace Caldwell, a friend of Marisa's. I don't see her car in the parking lot. Is she home sick today?"

The woman's smile fell away. Crashed, actually.

Ace's adrenaline jacked. Something had happened to Marisa. Something bad. "What's wrong? Is she okay?"

"As far as I know, she's fine, but Marisa doesn't work here anymore."

Ace did a slow blink, stupefied. "She doesn't?"

"No. We had some cutbacks and..." The woman began to withdraw. "It really isn't my place to discuss this. Maybe you should give her a call."

"I'll do that." Stunned, bewildered, Ace pivoted on his boots.

Marisa had lost her job. She'd said nothing about it last night because she didn't want to worry Chance.

No wonder she'd been upset.

MARISA DIDN'T KNOW what she was going to do.

With a moan, she leaned an elbow on the tiny round dining table and stared at her new budget. No matter how she manipulated the numbers, she was in big trouble.

Earlier today, she'd applied for work in three places and filled out four more online applications, but none had seemed promising. The hours at Kids' Care had blended perfectly with her job at Sunset Manor. Where else would she find an employer so accommodating? It wasn't as if

LINDA GOODNIGHT

she was in high demand. Other than her nurse's aide certification, she had no job skills.

She had nowhere to turn except God, and she almost felt ashamed to bother Him now. For the past year, she'd let work and worry crowd out their relationship. Her fault.

Chest burdened to the point of rupture, she began to whisper a prayer, letting all the fear and anxiety tumble out in the empty room. Except it wasn't empty. Jesus had promised never to leave nor forsake her, and she'd clung to that promise from foster care into adulthood.

Tears dripped onto the yellow notepad with little *plop*s. A louder noise broke through her prayers.

Someone was at the door. Probably the mailman with another certified letter from a collection agency.

The day couldn't get worse. Might as well get this over with.

Heaving a sigh as heavy as her heart, Marisa blotted her face and went to answer.

Ace stood on her concrete slab. She didn't have the energy to slam the door in his face. Truth was, she needed a friend.

Without saying a word, she stepped back and held the door open. Ace, all lean, muscled six feet of him, came right in.

He towered over her, and though she tried to keep him from seeing her red, watery eyes, he saw anyway.

He touched her tear-stained cheek. His tone tender enough to break her, he said, "I heard about the job. Are you okay?"

Too down to ask how he'd heard, she uttered a wobbly whisper. "No."

Marisa didn't know how it happened, but in the next instant, she was in Ace's arms. His long fingers cupped the back of her head. He stroked the other hand up and down her back, soothing as she would one of her daycare kids. But the kids weren't hers anymore.

The tears threatened to start up again. "I don't know what I'm going to do." The words were muffled against his shirt.

"How can I help? Anything you need. I'll do it." His tone was soft and ragged, full of emotion that went straight to her heart.

For once, she wasn't angered by his offer of help. She was touched. Ace was being kind, and she appreciated the effort. But she'd been on her own forever. No use getting clingy now and expecting more than he could give.

She drew away from his comforting presence but instantly wished to be back in his arms. Though she'd never expected to think such a thing again, Ace offered a strong, solid security she desperately needed. She'd never needed anyone.

"There's nothing you can do." Even though she wished there was. "No one seems to be hiring unskilled labor."

"You can use the break, Marisa. You're exhausted."

The statement drove her over the edge. Despair and frustration forced words out of her mouth. Naturally a man like Ace wouldn't understand.

"Don't you get it? Without this month's paycheck, I can't afford to pay for Chance's care. He'll be forced to move out of Sunset Manor!"

As soon as the words hit the air, Marisa dropped her head backwards and groaned. She hadn't wanted Ace to know how dire the situation was. "Forget I said that. Things will work out. They always do."

He couldn't possibly understand her plight. He'd always had job security, money, and a family to lean on.

Ace took hold of her upper arms. "I don't think so. Otherwise, you wouldn't be this distraught. Tell me all of it."

"I said, we will be fine." But she felt herself weakening.

He gazed down into her eyes long enough to make her squirm. He knew she was lying. A twinge of guilt poked at her conscience. She hated being lied to.

He tugged her toward the sofa. "Tell me. Together, we'll figure this out."

Part of her still feared trusting Ace Caldwell, but the other part was desperate to find answers for her brother. Chance came first, above her fears, above her bizarre, unshakable attachment to this cowboy.

As she lowered to the couch, the worn piece of furniture sagged in the middle. She scooted to one end. The cushion rode up. Ace smashed it down as he sat beside her.

He didn't, she noticed for the hundredth time, smell like beer. That much she could trust. He smelled of pressed cotton shirt and woodsy cologne. And cinnamon. She'd always loved the way he smelled just as she loved the way he held her. When he wasn't drinking.

If she could only believe he'd changed for good. Her parents never had, though they'd promised dozens of times through the years.

"Everything's such a mess." She was confused, worried, and broke. How much worse could it get?

ACE LISTENED as Marisa finally shared her burdens. They were many and serious. Most he knew from the private investigator's report, although hearing them from her, knowing she trusted him enough to talk, patched a hole in his chest.

When she blurted her worries about Chance and got all glassy-eyed again, he moved near enough to get his arm around her shoulders. She stiffened only for a moment before tilting her head against his side. She needed him, and it felt good. He dropped a kiss on her hair, a kiss of compassion and connection, expecting nothing in return. No agenda. No strings attached.

He wasn't that guy anymore.

His heart ached for this strong woman who'd fought the world by herself every day of her life. How could he make her understand that she didn't have to be alone anymore?

Words wouldn't suffice. She only trusted actions, and his hadn't been stellar for too long.

Trust broken took a long time to rebuild, but he was up for the challenge. He wanted Marisa to lean on him. He wanted to be her hero.

He asked a few questions here and there, but eventually she ran dry and went silent. They sat together on the saggy old couch, his head resting on hers and hers against his side. She fit so beautifully this way that he never wanted to move.

But he had to. Problems wouldn't resolve themselves while he admired Marisa's soft hair and feminine curves.

Redirecting his thoughts, he prayed for wisdom and direction. The only answer that occurred to him would probably make her mad, but he was a man of action, a problem solver. That's why he was CEO of a spread as big as The Triple C even though Nate was the oldest. Nate was hands-on with the animals and understood them better than Ace ever would. Management was Ace's style and strength. Right now, he wanted to put those skills to work.

"I have a plan," he said. "We'll move him to the ranch."

"*What?*" Marisa jerked upright and scooted all the way to the end of the couch, gray eyes wide.

Maybe he should have worked his way up to the ranch suggestion.

Bringing his knee up on the now protruding couch cushion, he pivoted in her direction. He'd rather she move close again, but from her horrified expression, she wasn't likely to do that any time soon.

"The ranch is the perfect solution. The guest house can be made accessible with minimal effort. We'll have it fixed up in no time, and the rent is free. He can live there."

"Do you realize how ridiculous that sounds? Who would take care of him?"

"You would, until he can handle things on his own." Ace was convinced Chance could be independent again. Other paras were. Why not Chance?

"In case you've forgotten, I have a job. Only one, but still a job that pays the bills." She winced. "*Some* of the bills. And buys food and gasoline and all the other little necessities you seem to have forgotten about."

"We'll figure it out. There are plenty of people on the ranch who can look out for Chance while you're at work."

Dark hair that moments before had brushed his cheek swished against her pink shirt. "No."

"Why? Because it's my idea?"

"Because no one else should be responsible for my brother except me."

"Why?"

"Would you stop asking me that question?"

An ornery grin tugged at his lips. He couldn't help himself. "Why?"

Marisa snarled at him and then chuckled. "Don't make me laugh. This is serious business."

"Yes, and my idea has value. You can't afford the care center, and Chance despises the place anyway." Ace took her hand. Her fingers lay loose and limp, but she didn't yank away. He took that as a good sign.

Drawing on the persuasive techniques he used to sell bulls for a premium price and negotiate cattle and land deals, he pressed his argument. "Don't you think he'd be happier on a ranch? Those folks at Sunset are nice people, but no one there is anywhere close to Chance's age."

"He could have friends visit if he wanted."

"But he doesn't want to. One"—Ace held up a finger —"he's embarrassed to live in a senior facility, and two"— he ticked up another finger—"he doesn't want anyone to view him as a cripple. We can fix both of those by moving him to the ranch."

Her laugh was harsh. "Oh, sure. Right. Do you think

he'll magically regrow his spinal cord just because he's on your ranch?"

"Look." Ace scooted a little closer. "He's been depressed and refused to assist in his own recovery. Right?"

"I'm afraid so."

"A change of scenery could make all the difference."

"A handicapped-accessible guest house doesn't solve everything, Ace."

"You need a solution right away, at least a temporary one. Think of my offer in that vein. As temporary. You can always change your mind after you find another job." And he'd do his best to convince her not to. "In the meantime, you'll have all day with your brother." And with me. "In the evenings, he can have dinner with us, hang with the family for a while, and then be sound asleep in the guest house when you get home."

She brushed a hand over the top of her head, pausing at the crown to stare at nothing and consider. He thought she might be weakening. "I don't know."

Ace pressed the advantage. "Free rent, fresh air and sunshine, and good friends all around him are the perfect solution. And he loves Connie's cooking."

He didn't add the rest. Not yet. Once she realized he was right, he'd share his other plans for her baby brother.

Marisa shot a glance at the round-faced watch she always wore and hopped up. "I have to go to work."

"I'll get out of here so you can get ready, but think about everything I said, okay?" He caught her hand again and squeezed. "Pray about it."

She licked her lips, a sure sign of uncertainty, and nodded. "Okay."

That was the best answer he'd get from her today. But Ace had made up his mind, and when he believed in something strong enough, he was a bulldozer.

CHAPTER 12

*M*arisa had thought life couldn't get any worse. As usual, she was wrong.

She fretted over Ace's suggestion the rest of the day and all during her shift at Sunset Manor. Chance must have asked her ten times to tell him what was wrong until she'd finally grown tired of the question and blurted out the truth. Not the part about being too broke to pay attention, but Ace's offer of the guest house.

Naturally, her brother had loved the idea and hadn't even bothered to ask why Ace would make such an offer. She wondered, though. This was way beyond soothing his conscience.

Chance had his own misguided thoughts. "He's in love with you."

"Don't be dumb. He's working through his Twelve Step program. We're part of his recovery."

"It's more than that." Chance pointed at her. "And I think you feel the same."

175

She might be in love with Ace, but she didn't dare take that risk again.

Still, she mulled the conversation and the guest house situation off and on all the next morning. One way or the other, she had to make new arrangements for Chance's care. The guest house at the Triple C Ranch seemed more of a fantasy than a workable reality, but she couldn't stop thinking about it. Especially after making three calls to various agencies in search of assistance for her brother and coming away empty. Even if Chance qualified, every agency had a long waiting list.

She pressed *end* on her cell phone and wandered out the back door to the single lawn chair to pray and think. She'd promised to do both.

The morning sun was nice. She stretched out her legs and gazed at the fluffy clouds floating overhead. Not a breath of air stirred, but she caught the sweet scent of the neighbor's mimosa trees.

If she agreed to Ace's crazy plan, she'd be living in daily contact with the cowboy she'd wanted to forget. She'd be obligated to him, an idea she didn't like at all. But she'd also have an opportunity to really observe him in his natural environment, not just when he was on his best behavior. She could learn if he'd really become the man he seemed to be, a man who had won her admiration. Chance was right about that. But that didn't mean she'd let down her guard. She understood her weakness, her predilection for unpredictable alcoholics.

She listed the pros of moving to the guest house. Free rent, both for her and Chance. She might even save some money. An environment that made Chance happier.

Opportunities for him to interact with friends closer to his age. Maybe he'd decide to reenter the world and invite his old friends over. Wouldn't that be something?

The move could be temporary if she chose. She wouldn't be stuck there permanently.

Plus, the ranch had a pool house. Water therapy for Chase, though even that scared her. How would he manage without legs? Ace probably had a plan for that, as well.

Then she listed the negatives. Obligation to other people. To Ace. The cowboy was the biggest issue. Marisa feared exposing her brother to danger again, either from the ranching environment or from Ace's influence.

Her phone buzzed. She glanced at Caller ID, not recognizing the number.

Hopeful that one of the agencies was calling with better news, she answered. "Hello."

"Marisa?"

Her heart tumbled to the bottom of her feet. Maybe lower. "Mom? Is that you?"

How had her mother gotten this number? She hadn't heard from Alene Foreman since right after Chance's accident. Mom had seen the news on the television and had come to the hospital, too drunk to be coherent. Her slobbery tears had been for herself, not for Chance. She'd even tried panhandling the nurses, pleading that her beloved son was now a "helpless cripple". Marisa had been so angry she'd had security escort her screeching mother out the door.

It had been the first she'd seen the woman in eight years, and she hadn't seen her father in even more.

"How you doin', baby girl?" Alene hiccoughed, giggled.

"Okay. You?" Besides being drunk or high.

"Oh, honey, you jus' don't know the half of it. I've been sick and had to quit my job."

Marisa rolled her eyes toward the blue sky. Since when had Alene held a job for more than a week? "Sorry to hear that."

"Well, see, I got kicked out of my house. It was a real nice place. Pool and everything."

Right. As if they'd ever lived in swanky digs. She'd probably been squatting in someone's empty house and gotten caught. They'd done that plenty before family services had rescued Marisa and Chance for the final time.

"So, what do you say, baby girl? Can Mama come stay with you awhile? Just 'til I get back on my feet?"

Revulsion crawled like ants over Marisa's skin. She hadn't lived with either of her parents since she was small, and for good reason. "Not a good idea, Mom."

Alene's voice turned to a whine. "I'm your mama. You owe me that much."

Marisa blurted the first thought that came to her mind. "I've lost my job, too, and I can't pay the bills. I have to move right away. By the end of the month. And we have nowhere to go."

In that moment, she made her decision. She and Chance were moving to The Triple C.

ACE EXITED the Baptist Church basement next to his mentee, Don, following an AA meeting.

He dropped a hand on the other man's shoulders. "Want to grab something to eat?"

"Not tonight, but thanks. It's my oldest boy's birthday." A fresh light beamed on Don's face. "Joanie invited me over for cake and ice cream."

"I thought you seemed pretty upbeat tonight. She's talking to you again?"

"I hope so. When I told her I'd be late, I think she wanted to withdraw the invitation. When I explained about the meeting and that I didn't want to miss one, she sounded...I don't know...relieved, I guess." He stuck a hand in his pants pocket and withdrew his car keys. "I've missed a lot of birthdays and messed up a few more. I won't let them down this time."

"Or ever again."

"That's the plan." He jiggled the keys. "You were right. It's getting easier. Life seems brighter."

"Even if she goes through with the divorce, you have to keep that attitude."

"I'm doing all I can to change her mind."

"I know the feeling." He was, he realized, doing all he could to change Marisa's mind about a lot of things. Mostly him. "Enjoy the party."

They both laughed. The word party had taken on a whole new connotation. Don lifted a hand and walked toward the bronze Mercedes parked toward the back of the lot.

Ace headed to his truck and thought about dropping by Marisa's house. It wasn't that late. She'd be home soon. He could wait in her driveway. A little conversation, some more reasons why she and Chance should move to the ranch, maybe a goodnight kiss.

On his way, he stopped at Braum's ice cream store. He was a plain vanilla man himself, but Marisa loved Rocky Road. It wouldn't hurt to sweeten her up with her favorite ice cream. He picked up both flavors and tossed the selections into a shopping cart.

He was hungry. Dinner had worn off during the cathartic stress of the AA meeting.

Studying the flavorings, Ace considered a jar of caramel sauce and maybe some pecans. Yeah, and bananas. Maybe they'd make sundaes together. He tossed all the items into the basket and had started to the checkout when he met Kristin Fairchild. He hadn't seen her since that night at Carla's Country Café when she'd come on strong enough to make his knees weak.

She was with another woman, this one a sporty looking brunette a head shorter than the model-like Kristin.

When his old party pal spotted him, she smiled her sexy, *I'm available* smile that had once drawn Ace to her faster than he could think. Truth was, he hadn't been thinking at all back then.

"Hello again, handsome. Long time no see."

She was another person on his list of apologies, even though he was no longer the least bit attracted to her. He wondered if Marisa had anything to do with his about-face.

They exchanged pleasantries. Kristin introduced her friend as Jasmine and invited Ace to join the two of them at a table.

"Can't, but thanks." He gestured toward the cart. "Ice cream. I don't want it to melt."

"Nice to meet you, Ace." Jasmine waved toward the counter. "I'm going to go ahead and order. What do you want, Kristin?"

Kristin gave her order, and the other woman walked away.

Kristin showed no signs of doing the same. She eased closer to Ace until he smelled her expensive perfume. "Looks like you're having a party."

"Just ice cream with a friend."

Kristin perched a hand on one hip. "And I'll bet my boots this friend is female."

"You'd win that bet."

"And you're buying her ice cream. Isn't that sweet? She must be someone pretty special for you to drive all the way to Clay City at this hour."

Special? Absolutely. "Marisa works the late shift. Doesn't get off until eleven."

"Marisa? Do I know her?"

Ace shrugged. "Maybe. Marisa Foreman. She went to Clay City High. Her brother's in the care center here, and he's a pal of mine. I visit him pretty often."

The accident that had paralyzed Chance was common knowledge, though he didn't expect Kristin to remember.

They continued the conversation for a few more minutes while he worried that the ice cream would melt. The checker rang up his purchases and he paid. Kristin stood at his side, chatting away.

Finally, he glanced at this cell phone. Almost eleven.

"I have to go. Nice seeing you."

"Let's get together soon."

He paused. Ice cream or not, he had to try. "Let's do that. Why don't you come to my church on Sunday? Evangel Church in Calypso. It's right on the main highway when you first come into town. Worship starts at 10:30. Sunday School at 9:30."

Kristin gave a nervous laugh and fluttered a hand. "I'm not much of a church-goer. You know that as well as anyone."

"I wasn't either until recently. Seriously. You should come."

Suddenly eager to escape, his party pal glanced over one shoulder to where Jasmine had found a table. "I'll think about it."

"You do that." But he wouldn't hold his breath.

"IT'S ONLY TEMPORARY." Marisa jabbed a finger at the two grinning males. Between her mother's phone call and Ace's late night house call, which had ended as sweetly as the ice cream had tasted, she was almost eager to make the move.

Ace lounged against the wall next to Chance's fish poster, arms crossed, looking as if he wanted to hug her. Or kiss her. Something he'd done only once last night. One gentle little kiss that had ended way too soon. If she closed her eyes, she could still taste the caramel on his lips.

As if he could read her mind, a smile curved those tempting lips. She blinked and turned her attention to her brother. He'd been bugging her ever since she'd told him of the offer. The pleasure and hope in his eyes made the decision easier.

Marisa was still scared out of her mind. But that was nothing new. She was always scared. She'd been scared since the first time Mom and Dad had left her alone with her new baby brother. For five days. She'd been seven.

"We're already doing the renovations." Ace unwound his long body from the wall to move toward her. "Should be ready by the end of the month. Want to come out and see?"

"Yes!" Chance pumped an arm. The one with the white bandage.

"Good," Ace said. "We'll go fishing, and I'll win back my bragging rights."

"In your dreams." Chance laughed. A happy, excited sound that almost chased her fears away.

Marisa turned the conversation back to the move. "I want to help with the renovations."

Ace looked at her as if she'd gone mad. "I have men for that."

"Are you saying a girl can't put up a towel bar?"

Ace held out both hands. "Hey, I have Emily and Connie in my family. They can do anything. You'll never find me questioning the abilities of a female. What I meant was, there's no need for you to trouble yourself."

"We want to, don't we, Chance?" If she was going to be obligated to the Caldwell family, particularly Ace, she could at least put in some sweat equity.

"Sounds fun to me. My arms are kind of wimpy." Chance pumped a pale bicep. "Time to get in shape."

"What time do the guys start working in the morning?"

"Early. Maybe six."

"We'll be there."

MOST SUMMERS, mid-June wasn't too hot, but the humidity could be a choker.

Ace wiped sweat from his face with a kerchief. Haying season was upon them, and with the extra work at the guest house, his men were overloaded. He'd called in a couple of experts for the guest house to free up his ranch hands. Even with more help, days were long and work was hard, hot, and sweaty.

He circled the tractor around the field four more times, watching in his mirror as the rake pulled the cut alfalfa into tidy windrows for drying. After the final hill was formed, he disengaged the rake and headed for the nearest barn. He was three miles from the big house, but he had a hankering to be there. With this field cut and raked, he could hop in his truck and head home for lunch.

So he did.

A plumber's van was parked outside the guest house. The new chair-accessible shower was being completed today. Marisa had had a fit when she'd found out that the renovations were a little more extensive than Ace had let on. He didn't care. Dad had built this cottage to live in while the big house was going up. The place was ready for an update.

Other trucks, including his brother's and several belonging to the summer hands, were already scattered on the grass outside the main house. Connie would be serving up lunch soon.

He exited his truck and turned in the direction of the cottage. Marisa and Chance wouldn't take a break unless he complained.

For the past five days, they'd arrived every morning around six and didn't leave until time for Marisa to go on duty at Sunset Manor. Already, he could see a difference in both of them, especially Chance. Color had returned to his skin and, though his arms were nowhere near their former bulk, they'd gotten strong enough for him to assist more in transferring from car to chair and back. At this rate, he'd soon be putting himself to bed, taking showers alone, maybe even driving again.

Marisa would pitch a hissy if she heard him say that. For reasons he understood too well, she couldn't let go of her fear that something bad would happen to her brother. Because it already had.

The pinch of responsibility came again, less intense today, but still there. Would he always feel indebted to Chance?

"Looking good in here," he said as he stepped inside the guest house. An open concept, the living room opened into the dining and kitchen areas with bedrooms off to the left divided by one large bathroom. The tile floors throughout were still in good shape, so they'd covered them with painter's drop cloths. The smooth, even surface was perfect for a man in a chair.

Marisa, wielding a roller infused with gray paint, looked over one shoulder. "I like this color."

"It almost matches your eyes."

Those beautiful eyes sparked. "Is that good or bad?"

"Definitely good. Are you ready for lunch?" He took the roller from her and resisted the urge to kiss the top of her head. A glob of gray paint stuck there.

"I brought a sandwich."

She said that every day, and every day they argued. "Save it. Connie cooked."

"We can't keep taking advantage of her hospitality."

"If you don't, you'll break her heart. You wouldn't want that, would you?"

She gave a frustrated growl and reclaimed the paint roller. "At least let me finish this wall."

"Where's Chance?"

"Back there with the plumber." She dipped the roller in a tray, swished it back and forth.

"I'll say hi and see how they're coming along." He moseyed through the short hall. The bathroom door had been removed for work access. Inside, Chance used a power screwdriver to attach a hand bar next to the commode. The plumber was inside the immense shower finalizing the fixture installations.

Ace waited until the machine noise subsided. "You boys are doing some fine work in here."

The plumber made one final adjustment and stepped out. Even with three men in the room, they could maneuver around, perfect for a wheelchair.

Chance practically glowed. "Get a load of that shower, Ace. It's got everything a man could need. A bench, shelves I can reach, an overhead *and* a handheld, and watch this."

He whipped the wheelchair around with more energy

than the electric screwdriver and wheeled inside the shower stall, rolling back and forth between the bench and the other wall.

"Plenty of room. And I can do it all myself. No more nurses ogling me while I shower."

The plumber guffawed. "Why would you complain about that?"

Chance snickered. "You haven't seen my nurses."

Ace interrupted. "Don't let your sister hear you say that."

Chance rolled out of the shower to the free-standing vanity and long counter space, again practicing the ease with which he could maneuver the chair. "Marisa doesn't count."

She did to Ace. "Connie's got lunch ready for all of us. You, too, Tom," he said to the plumber. "Take a break."

"You don't have to tell me twice." Chance spun out of the room.

Ace met Marisa in the hall. She wore a bemused expression. "What did you say to him?"

He offered his most innocent shrug. "Lunch?"

Marisa chuckled and whacked him on the chest. He caught her hand, kissed the fingers, happy and at peace to have her here where he could do everything in his power to make her life better. Even if she remained only a few months, having her on the ranch smoothed the rough edges of guilt. Nothing could ever erase what had happened, but he couldn't live without her forgiveness.

He was starting to wonder if he could live without her at all.

CHAPTER 13

They moved in on a Thursday, Marisa's day off from Sunset Manor. Chance was so ramped-up he was like a Jack Russell Terrier on speed.

Marisa unpacked boxes in the newly refurbished kitchen as Ace and his hands, as he called the half dozen handsome cowboys who worked for him, hauled cartons inside the guest house. The men jostled and joked and sweated, delivering all her worldly goods much faster than she'd been able to pack them. In feeble exchange for their thoughtfulness and considerable muscle, she dispensed large, icy glasses of lemonade. Definitely worth the effort. Watching cowboys gulp it down could put a song in any girl's heart. Especially when Ace was one of those cowboys.

The men traipsed out again, leaving behind the empty glasses. She watched them go, thankful. Part of her was still scared of making a mistake, but, in this case, her choices had been too limited to fight the move. Another part of her recognized God's hand in the invitation. Her Heavenly Father had come to her rescue, and if He'd chosen to use Ace Caldwell to do it, who was she to argue? It was this she tried to cling to, though her fear of leaning on anyone kept poking its head up like an annoying gopher.

She poured herself a glass of the remaining lemonade and sipped, the tart sweetness a remedy to today's heat.

The guest house was small but adequate. In spite of her misgivings, she loved it, loved the clean freshness of everything, the tidiness.

She didn't even mind the odor of paint and plumbing glue that lingered in the rooms though the air conditioning ran full blast, thanks to all the open doors. What she did mind was being obligated, but when her brother sailed through the front door, alight with barely suppressed joy and a box balanced on his lap, she put her anxiety aside. She was doing this for Chance. He was worth it.

BY DAY three of life on the Triple C, Marisa had begun to relax and enjoy the quiet beauty of country living. The boxes were unpacked, clothes and household goods were put away, and at the moment, Whitney was helping hang curtains and pictures.

In Nate's bride, Marisa had discovered a surprising kindred spirit. Though Whitney had never been in foster care, she'd been on her own since she was a seventeen-year-old runaway. She'd known hard times. She also understood Marisa's powerful need for independence that conflicted with an equally powerful fear of being all alone against a harsh world.

Whitney slid a pocket curtain onto a rod. "How are you adjusting to life in the country? The noises bothered me at first."

"I've been so tired every night, I hardly notice them." She raised a hammer and pounded a curtain hook into the wall. "But it's a good tired. I sleep better knowing my brother is in the next room."

"He seems to be doing great, Marisa."

True, he was.

Chance had acclimated far faster and better than she'd expected. Last night, he'd insisted on showering and transferring from chair to bed and back without assistance. She'd been scared silly, but he'd relegated her to the hall, promising to holler if he needed help. He hadn't. And for two weeks now, ever since they'd begun coming to the ranch to work on the house, he'd been out of bed from morning until night, a vast change from the depressed, lethargic, bed-bound man he'd been in the care center. His thrill of doing things for himself made Marisa ashamed of the many times she'd taken her physical independence for granted.

She bit her bottom lip. "Sometimes I think I've been holding him back."

"You've done what you thought was best." Whitney squeezed her arm. "But isn't it nice to have other people on your team to help out now?"

"I worry he'll push too hard or too far and get hurt again."

"Not with the Caldwell machine surrounding him."

"It's the Caldwell machine that worries me. I've never had to lean on anyone before. I don't like the feeling." And her feelings for Ace were worrisome, too.

"That's because you're scared they'll let you down." Whitney handed over the curtain.

"They will. People always do. Chance and I have depended on no one except each other all our lives. We don't like it."

"Does Chance feel that way? Or is it just you?"

Marisa opened her mouth and closed it again. Was Whitney right? Was she the problem?

She turned toward the window and raised the rod to the wall. Whitney stepped up beside her.

"Let me hold one end and you take the other."

Together, the women snapped the curtain onto the newly hung hooks.

When they'd finished and backed up to survey their handiwork, Whitney pressed the subject. "Can I give you a bit of advice from someone who understands, at least a little, about how you feel?"

Warily, Marisa nodded. "I guess. As Ace says, you're probably going to anyway."

"He's right. So here it is." Whitney picked up another curtain and began threading it onto the rod. "If you're anything like me, and I think you are, you've got a wall up around your heart as high as Mount Everest. You'll never heal or have the one thing you want most in your life until you let down that guard."

What did she want most in life? Love. Family. Home. A man she could trust.

She rifled through a box of curtain hangers, hunting for the perfect nail.

"Ace is an alcoholic." Where had that come from?

"I wondered when we'd talk about that."

Marisa lifted her gaze from the box. "You knew?"

"All of us do. The Caldwell clan, I mean. We don't discuss it outside the family. Caldwells are private that way, but we're part of his recovery. I think you are too."

"I am. But not in the way you mean."

"No? I think you're wrong. I think you care about him, too, but he let you down. He hurt you. I get that."

"He hurt my brother."

"Did he?"

"Yes." Or had he? Chance, as he'd reminded her more than once, was a grown man. He'd made his choices.

Whitney blew out an annoyed breath and removed the curtain from the rod. She'd put it on backwards.

"Ace is the real deal, Marisa. He's working hard to be a better man and to prove to you and everyone else, maybe even to himself, that he's changed. I didn't know him before, but Nate talks to me. Ace never embraced his faith before. He's always struggled with spiritual questions, particularly about his mother's death. And he's such a strong, smart, capable man. He figured he could handle everything by himself. Why bother with God?"

"But the alcohol was stronger."

"For a while, I suppose. The accident shook him up. As horrible as it is to think, the Bible says God can bring good out of bad if we let Him."

"What good can possibly come from my brother being

paralyzed?" The thought was still a bitter taste on her tongue.

"I'm not saying God caused the accident. We make our own choices. But God, in His mercy and love, will always redeem a situation if we're willing to let Him. He did for me."

"What do you mean?"

"I made a lot of dumb, rebellious choices as a teenager. *I* chose to abandon a good home and good parents. *I* chose to run away and live with guys who mistreated me. God didn't choose my lifestyle. I did. Mostly, I chose to ignore God until my babies' lives were at stake."

"Seriously? Your twins?"

"It's hard to even think about now, but my ex didn't want kids, and told me to take care of the problem. I stumbled into a Christian clinic and found Jesus, instead. And then, He led me here."

"Thank God."

"I do. Every day. But I had a choice. That's what I'm saying to you. Choices. We all have them."

"Why did it have to be Chance? He was always a good kid."

"I don't have all the answers, Marisa. No one does. Sometimes bad stuff happens to good people. It's just part of this crazy world. We don't always understand the unfairness of life." She put her palms together, prayer-like. "All I know is this: I once was lost and now I'm found. I have peace with God that no circumstance can take away. Even in terrible situations, Christ followers can find joy in Him. It's not easy, and we have to fight for it, but fighting for peace and joy is so much better than living with anxiety and fear."

Emotion welled in Marisa. She agreed with everything Whitney was saying. "I don't know how to do that. I wish I did."

"Then start with one thing at a time. *Choose* to be happy here. Choose to be at peace with this big, loving family who wants to embrace you and Chance."

Marisa breathed in, settling something deep inside. "I think I can do that."

Whitney toted the rethreaded curtain to the window. "Ace may not fully know why he invited you here. But the rest of us can see that it's more than helping out a friend or completing a Twelve-Step program."

"I've wondered." More than wondered. She'd felt the vibes. Because she had them, too.

"If you have any feelings for him at all, find a way to trust him again, and then decide what you want or don't want. Don't let fear control your choices. Believe me, the Caldwell men are worth it."

THE SUN HAD YET to break the horizon when Marisa awoke. Months of getting up at five o'clock had ingrained the habit. She rose and dressed while coffee brewed, then took a cup out on the railed porch to watch the ranch come to life.

In such a short time, it had become a new habit, this quiet time alone while Chance slept on, resting better than he had since before the accident. Ace said it was because he spent the day in activity. Truly, one Caldwell or the other always seemed to desire her brother's help or his company. At first, she'd been anxious, but taking Whitney's advice, she'd forced her guard to lower, perhaps not all the way, but enough to let Chance out of her sight. The *what-ifs* stuck in the back of her mind like a parasite.

True to his word, Ace had worked out a schedule so that Chance was seldom alone even though he insisted he could manage. This was a new side of her brother, a side she hadn't seen since before the accident. Hopeful. Brighter. Almost eager for life.

Each time she drove to Clay City to work, she breathed a little easier. Everything was going well. Almost too well. She hoped she wasn't in for another ugly surprise.

Cupping her hands around the warm mug, Marisa leaned against the white wood railing. In front of her, across perhaps fifty yards, was the back and side of the main house. Already, the ant-like activity had begun to stir. Men would arrive, some would share in the Caldwell breakfast, and all would receive their work assignments from the big boss, Ace Caldwell.

Watching him in action impressed her. She'd never understood how hard he worked. To her, he'd been the rich cowboy without a serious thought. She'd been wrong. He ran a small empire with smooth expertise and still carved out time for her and Chance, church and friends, helping neighbors, and many other things. Did he ever sleep?

Two pickup trucks pulled in, doors slammed, and voices broke the morning quiet. Nate went inside.

Beck, one of the permanent ranch employees, saw her as he exited his truck and lifted a hand. She saluted him with her cup. As Beck disappeared inside the house, to the office, she assumed, another cowboy came out.

Her heart executed a dandy little jitterbug. Hatless, his black hair a tad unruly, Ace crossed the backyard and the service road that divided them, coming to stand in front of her.

"Good morning. Why are you up so early?"

"Habit. But I love this time of day."

"Yeah. Me too. Some people dread getting up with the sun." He pivoted so his profile was towards her as he dipped his chin toward the horizon. "To me, the sunrise means a fresh, clean start, a brand new twenty-four hours. It's as if God rubs his hand across the world and gives us another chance to get it right."

Marisa listened, the cup warm in her hands, touched by the depth of his words. Another chance. Was that what he was asking of her? And if God gave second chances, shouldn't she be willing to do the same?

"That's lovely, Ace. Almost poetic."

He turned back to face her, abashed. "Yeah, well, mornings do that to me. Especially in the presence of a beautiful woman. Which brings me to my reason for being here."

He stepped up on the porch, close enough that his fresh-shaved scent mingled pleasantly with her coffee.

His eyes, made greener by an olive shirt, were serious and searching. "Take a ride with me. I want to show you something."

"Now?"

"The best time of the day."

"What about your ranch hands?"

"Taken care of."

"Chance is still asleep."

"Not a problem. Nate and Whitney have something going for him this morning."

"Oh, that's right. He wanted to see Whitney's miniatures."

"And Whitney needs him to do some painting."

"Seriously?" Okay, that sounded doable, safe. Chance enjoyed being productive, and miniature animals couldn't knock him over. "His arms are starting to look like they used to when he was coaching."

"I noticed. The exercise is good for him."

It was. She couldn't deny it. "He's thriving, Ace. I owe you that."

He took her coffee cup and sipped. "Then take a ride with me."

"I need my coffee first."

His teeth flashed. He returned the cup. "I'll grab a couple of travel mugs from the house and meet you at the truck."

"Okay." His truck was parked in the garage at the back of the house, directly in line with her porch. Rather, the guest-house porch. The word *guest* was a good reminder than her presence here was temporary.

But Whitney's advice was never far from her thoughts. Ace had been nothing but good to her and her brother this time around. Maybe he deserved a second chance.

Ace pointed his truck down the driveway and onto the adjoining roadway, though every inch of property for miles on both sides of the gravel road belonged to the Caldwell family.

At his side where he wanted her to be, Marisa sat in the passenger seat sipping coffee from a stainless-steel Yeti tumbler.

"May I ask where we're going?"

"You'll see when we get there."

"You're being mysterious." She shot him a grin. "Should I be scared?"

No, but he was. "Some things are better shown than told."

They rode a few miles in quiet companionship, and that felt right too. When he spotted three deer in one of the fields, peacefully grazing on his alfalfa, he pointed. She gasped with pleasure, her pretty face bright, and emitted a low, sweet, "Oh."

It was all he could do not to stop the truck and kiss her.

A man could get used to seeing Marisa's face every morning.

"Morning is the best time to see wild game. Especially where we're going."

She turned a soft smile in his direction. "I get the feeling this is somewhere special."

Ace had missed this side of Marisa. Behind her anger and sorrow, she'd hidden the gentle woman he'd been in love with. This morning, her guard was down, and he hoped she'd stay this way.

Marisa had been the one woman who'd really gotten

LINDA GOODNIGHT

him. She'd once told him his drinking was a Band-Aid, and under the Band-Aid was a tender, loving man he wanted to hide. Ace didn't want to hide anymore. Especially from her.

He made the turns, his wheels stirring late June dust, and after ten minutes, the open pastures and grain fields gave way to thick woods. This was his destination, a nearly sacred piece of Caldwell land. He'd never shared it with another soul.

He parked, jumped out, and using his key, unlocked the wide iron gate emblazoned with the Triple C. He pushed it open and smiled when Marisa slid into the driver's seat and drove through.

After relocking the gate, he reached for the door handle, but she pulled a few feet ahead, grinning at him through the closed glass. Each time, he tried to open the door, she moved the truck. Laughing, he jogged alongside the slowly moving vehicle until she took pity and let him in.

"You'll pay for that." But his threat only brought more laughter.

"Remember when you did that to me?"

"Did I?" He pretended innocence.

Marisa widened her eyes. They sparkled with ornery pleasure. "Like, maybe a dozen times."

"Payback is tough."

"Remember that, mister, or I'll have you jogging all over Calypso County."

"Two can play at that game. This is my truck."

"The gauntlet has been thrown. The battle is on."

They continued the banter, a light, joyous feeling

200

permeating the truck cab. She was happy this morning, and that made him happy. He wanted to keep her that way.

Ace drove forward a few hundred yards, taking it easy down a rugged, grassy path, and parked the truck in a clearing inside a stand of sweetgum and oak. Tall, narrow trees stretched toward the sky, their leafy heads filled with the twitters of birdsong. Willow Creek babbled to their right, a watering hole for all sorts of critters. The grass, littered with twigs and leaves, sparkled with the morning dew.

They got out and Marisa gazed around, interested the way he'd hoped.

"What is this place?"

He took her hand. Soft, warm, accepting. "Five hundred acres of untamed wilderness. It's ours, but we don't cultivate or graze here."

"A refuge?"

"For man as well as animals. I come here when I want to be alone to think or pray. All the family does. We call it the Sanctuary."

"I can understand why." She turned to face him. "It's so...peaceful and beautiful, as if God is here."

A cold place inside him that never seemed warm enough heated. She'd voiced exactly the way he felt. "This is where I met Him."

"God?"

"Yeah." He glanced aside, uncomfortable, but needing her to know the whole, ugly-to-beautiful truth. "When I hit rock bottom and knew I had to make a change, I came here. Spent two nights and days, mostly sitting right over there by the creek."

Her gaze followed his nod to a boulder beneath a weeping willow. She moved in that direction, pulling him along until they stood in the very spot where he'd surrendered his soul, his life, the alcohol and all the ugliness buried deep inside him.

He watched as she stood beside the clear creek and gazed at the sun rays beginning to slice between the tree trunks. Would she understand why this place was so important?

The answer was crucial for reasons he couldn't articulate.

They stood so quietly, lost in thoughts, that half a dozen wild turkeys waddled down the opposite bank to drink and flutter their wings. Squirrels chattered from the trees or darted through the leaves, their tails swept up in twitching question marks.

Barely moving his head, Ace exchanged a secret smile with Marisa. No words were needed. This was, indeed, a sanctuary.

After a peaceful while, he said, "Let's walk."

"All five hundred acres?"

He tilted his head with a smile. "Why not?"

She fell in step with him, picking over fallen tree limbs. "What made your family decide to set aside so much land for nature?"

"My mother."

"You don't talk much about her."

"I don't remember her very well. Bits and pieces of vague memory are all I have, but Dad was devoted to her until the day he died. He preserved this for Mom, at her request." He stooped, picked up a blue feather and handed it to Marisa. "After she was diagnosed with cancer, she came here a lot."

"I can see why. With all she was going through, she must have felt some measure of comfort here."

"When she got too weak to come, Dad carried her out here. He never told me that, but Gilbert did."

"He loved her very much."

"So much that he never remarried, though he had plenty of offers over the years. He said Cori was his one and only. That they were like the lone white dove she discovered out here one day." He plucked a leaf, studied it. "Doves mate for life. Did you know that?"

"If I did, I've forgotten."

"I think Dad regretted the time he hadn't spent with her."

Twigs snapped beneath their feet. A redbird flashed between the trees.

"What makes you think so?"

"My father was a driven man. A good, godly man, but a workaholic. When he did something, he did it with everything he had."

"Sounds like someone I know."

"Gilbert says the same thing." Ace, like his father, was driven, except his father had channeled his passion into building the Triple C. He'd been a workaholic, not an alcoholic. The difference stabbed Ace like a knife. He'd let his dad down, too. "I don't mind taking after Dad, especially if I can learn to be as generous and wise as he was. Nate's like Mom, in love with the land and the animals."

LINDA GOODNIGHT

"And what are you in love with?"

You. But he didn't say that. Instead, he continued walking, his boots crunching leaves underfoot. When they broke into another clearing, he stopped.

Marisa came up beside him. "What is this?"

"Cori's Chapel. Dad built it for her when she first got sick."

"No wonder she came here to pray. It's beautiful."

Almost reverently, they approached the tiny wooden church. The copse around it was wild and natural, a sprawling tangle of honeysuckle and blackberry vines. Even from a distance, the honeysuckle scented the air with sweet perfume.

The chapel door was unlocked, as it always was, and they went inside. Sunlight beamed through the windows and the skylight onto four wooden pews of polished oak, glossy and beautiful in their simplicity. A matching oak altar stretched across the front. Against the back wall, above all else, hung a rough-hewn wooden cross.

Ace took a seat on the front pew and was gratified when Marisa sat close to him. He loved everything about this chapel. Though he'd run from God most of his life, God had always been here.

"This is the one place I feel as if I know my mother."

"I'm sorry you never really knew her." She fiddled with the blue feather while she looked at him.

He took it from her, slid it into her hair behind one ear. Blue looked pretty against her glossy hair. "I have pictures of the two of us together when I was small." A beautiful young black-haired woman reading to him, rocking him, feeding him. He'd gotten his coloring from her. Green eyes, black hair, dark skin. "I think about those photos when I'm here and imagine I can remember."

"Maybe you do. Some part of you anyway." She lifted his hand from the smooth oak and laced their fingers together. "Your mother was a fine woman. She loved you. If she could have stayed and raised you, she would have. Not all mothers want to stay."

She spoke of herself, and the truth of that fact seared Ace's heart. He was scarred by the loss of his mother to cancer at such a young age. She and Chance had been deeply scarred by parents who were still alive and yet had chosen their addiction over their children. The pain of that betrayal must cut deeper than anything he could ever understand.

And he had added to her wounds with his own addiction.

Ace shifted on the bench, turning to the woman who touched him like no other. "I'm sorry."

She had no idea how sorry.

Marisa shook her head. "I've dealt with it. Mostly."

He wasn't speaking only of her parents. "And done a great job of it, too."

"Sometimes I wonder if I have. I get so confused, and all the ugly memories come back to me, especially at night when I'm alone. I was always scared. Sometimes I still am. I wanted her to come for me so badly, I ached, but she never did. So many times, I'd stare out the door or the window, waiting, waiting. Today would be the day. Today. For sure." She heaved a heavy, heartrending sigh. "It's a horrible feeling, knowing your mother doesn't love you. At least, not enough to be there."

"It still hurts you." Every protective instinct in him wanted to wrap her in his arms and never let anyone hurt her again. Not her mother nor her father nor even himself. Especially himself.

She made a soft sound. "Aren't we a pair, the two of us?"

"A good pair, I hope." He covered their joined hands with his other one. His fingers were dark against her much paler skin. He liked the contrast.

She didn't reply to his comment, and he let it go. This was not the place for romantic overtures. He hadn't come here for that.

Why *had* he brought her to the Sanctuary?

But he knew, and he had to leave the rest to God.

"Do you mind if we pray before we walk some more?"

Her beautiful mouth curved, lighting her eyes from within. "I'd like that very much."

$\mathcal{M}$arisa soaked in the tranquil woods and the complex cowboy walking beside her. Ace was different in his sanctuary. And for the first time, her eyes had been opened to a truth she'd never considered. He, too, had suffered loss. He, too, ached with an emptiness that could never be satisfied, no matter how much money he had or how charmed his life appeared to be. Like her, he'd suffered a mother wound. The acknowledgement made her feel closer to him.

They'd prayed together. She couldn't get over the emotion of kneeling at that altar, her hands clasped with Ace's, both their spirits lifted toward heaven. A holy moment, it had connected her to this cowboy in a way nothing else could have.

Now, hand on her elbow, a quiet, thoughtful Ace led her around to the side of the tiny chapel to a gravesite.

She knew before they approached the stone and read the names. "Your parents."

"Mom asked to be buried here, and of course, Dad wanted to be next to her."

Marisa rubbed her fingers over the shiny black granite topped by a pair of white doves. "Who chose the stone?"

"Dad."

Marisa traced the birds, their heads together, the small one snuggled against the larger one.

"Doves," she said softly, and thought how tragic and romantic the gesture had been.

"Mated for life."

Her eyes flashed to his. "That's beautiful."

"I think so too." He squatted to pluck weeds from around the base. "I want the same thing. When the time is right."

Her heart stilled. "Want what?"

He looked up at her, holding her gaze until her throat filled with emotion. "A love like my parents had, one that doesn't end."

"I've always wondered if love like that is possible."

His eyes never leaving hers, Ace rose, a few straggly weeds falling from his fingers.

Marisa took one step closer, surprising herself. His eyes widened, but he took another step until they were heart to heart.

"Love is what two people decide to make it." His face moved closer and closer to hers.

Her body tingled with wanting him. "Is that what's happening between us?"

"I never wanted our break up." He shook his head, expression haunted. "Never wanted to be away from you or to cause you grief or—"

She placed a finger on his tempting lips. His warm breath blew goosebumps down her arms. "Me either."

"You didn't?"

"No." The admission made her vulnerable, but she'd recalled Whitney's advice and said it anyway, believing, truly believing in this moment that Ace was sincere.

The morning ebbed around them, the nearby song of Willow Creek a serenade.

Ace cupped her face with his strong rancher's fingers. "Maybe we could start again."

Marisa tilted her head, relishing his touch. She felt cherished, loved. "Like this morning's sunrise. A clean slate."

"But wiser and better. I care about you, Marisa. Never stopped."

Then as if he couldn't wait another second, he kissed her. The kiss was restrained and tender, almost reverent as though her feelings, more than his desire, mattered most.

Marisa slid both arms around him and pulled him as close as her next breath. She loved this man. With all his faults and mistakes, he was a good person. He'd tried his best to prove it, and she wanted to believe in him.

Maybe it was time to let go of the past and reach for the future.

For a moment, she shut off the tumble of thoughts and doubts and sorrow and enjoyed the man, taking pleasure in his pleasure, loving that she was here with him.

When the kiss ended, too soon, it seemed to her, Ace continued to bracket her cheeks with both hands, his slight smile tender.

Her mouth curved in response. An aching sweetness filled her, filled the humming air around them. "Strange place to kiss a girl."

"I think my parents would approve." He placed another kiss on the corner of her mouth and let her go. She was sorry about that. "As much as I'd like to stay here all day, we both have work."

In mutual agreement, arms around each other's waists, they walked the distance back to the truck. She had no idea how long they'd been here. She wasn't wearing her watch, and she'd left her phone behind.

She stopped dead still. Adrenaline surged through her veins. Her contented haze evaporated.

"What's wrong?"

"I left my phone. Chance can't call me. What if—?"

Ace's long fingers squeezed her side, gentle and reassuring. "Stop worrying. I have my phone. If he needs something, he'll call, or Nate will." He tapped his forehead against hers. "He's fine. Are you?"

She gave a nervous little laugh. "I'm not used to anyone else watching out for him."

"He's a man, Marisa. You've got to turn him loose and let him discover how far he can go."

"I know. I know. But it's hard."

They walked on, quiet and contemplative until they reached the truck. Ace opened the passenger door. "You're still worried."

She bit her lip. "I don't want to be."

Ace's big hands bracketed her waist and lifted her into the truck seat. The courtesy wasn't necessary, but she didn't complain. He was a man. Men needed to do things for the people they cared about.

And he cared about her. She believed that now.

As he shut the door with a sharp snick and came around the truck, she realized what she'd been thinking. If Ace needed to do certain things because he was a man, didn't Chance need that, too?

Ace climbed into the driver's seat, shut the door and cranked the engine.

"I've always thought of Chance as a boy." She angled toward him. "My baby brother."

One arm slung across the back of the seat, Ace backed up and turned the truck toward the trail. As his body shifted back to the steering wheel, he looked at her. "He wants you to let him be a man, but he doesn't want to upset you."

"Did he tell you that?"

"In so many words." One hand to the wheel, he grasped her fingers with the other. "You've got to let him, sweetheart. For both of you."

"You're right. I know you're right." Being afraid that the sky would fall again hadn't made things any better. Nor would it keep bad things from happening.

Knowing this did not make letting go any easier.

They rode along in silence. Ace stared out the windshield, and Marisa stared at him. He was so handsome. But more than looks, he was substance. Another new revelation. Ace Caldwell was a solid, stable guy.

He pointed to where a doe, grazing with her fawn, lifted her head and watched them rumble past.

Contentment like she'd not known in ages, maybe ever, filtered through Marisa.

"Since you're thinking about Chance," Ace flashed her a glance. "I need to talk to you about something."

She hadn't been. She'd been thinking about him, about how good it felt to let herself be in love. "Okay. What is it?"

"He wants to do some things, and he's concerned about your reaction."

A frisson of tension tightened her shoulders. "What kind of things?"

Ace glanced at her and then back to the roadway. "He wants to ride again."

"Horses?" The idea shot terror from her head to her feet.

Ace's mouth tipped in sarcasm. "No. He wants to ride stick ponies."

"I could probably go for that."

"We have some dog-gentle horses that would be perfect, Marisa. Did you know there's a paraplegic girl who competes in barrel races?"

"Really?"

"Look her up. Her name is Amberley. She was in a wreck, too, but she's never let that stop her. She posts YouTube videos called *Wheelchair Wednesday*. Chance has been watching them, and he gets all revved up watching what she's accomplished. I think we can rig up the seatbelt and leg straps the same way she does."

"You're already thought this through, haven't you? Both of you?"

"He's thrilled about the possibility. Think about it, Marisa. On a horse, he'll have legs again."

She pressed her lips together, aching for her brother.

He'd have legs again. "But he could fall or the horse could stumble."

"All true. But he could also feel free and independent again. He needs this, Marisa. He's got big dreams."

"Not rodeo. He cannot ever think about that."

Ace chuckled. "He thinks if he can ride again, he can do other sports, and then he can coach again. He wants to relearn to drive too."

"That's not possible."

"Sure it is. There's a guy in Calypso in a chair, and he drives anywhere he wants to go. Alone. The car has hand controls. With some additional upper body strength for lifting the chair in and out of the car, Chance could do it, too."

"It sounds crazy and dangerous to me. I don't know how any of this could be possible. He's paralyzed, Ace. If he falls or gets in a bind, he can't get himself out."

"Let him try, Marisa. Give him your blessing. It's all he wants." He squeezed her hand. "He loves you, you know."

She glanced at her handsome cowboy, suddenly suspicious. "Was this a set up? Taking me to your sanctuary, the sweetness, the tender words?" The love she'd felt from and for him.

His face fell. "Seriously? You think that?"

Did she? She pondered less than a second. "No. I don't."

That was the crux of the matter. She'd always believed him, even when she shouldn't have. And she wanted to believe him now. She only hoped he wouldn't let her down again.

CHANCE STARTED RIDING lessons that very evening.

Ace was proud of him. Proud of Marisa too. She'd spoken to her brother after their trip to the Sanctuary and offered her blessing. It had been a cautious offering, fraught with warnings to start slow and build up to actually getting on a horse. Ace had seen her anxiety, but she'd done it. For Chance. Maybe for Ace. Anyway, he liked to think that.

Their time at the Sanctuary stayed with him all day. He was in love with her, and she was willing to give him a second chance. He loved her more deeply because of that. He deserved nothing, but oh, he was thankful.

"Hey, are we gonna do this, or are you going to daydream?" Chance's voice broke through his reverie.

"This daydream I'm having is mighty tempting."

"About my sister?"

"Maybe. Wise guy." Ace lifted the saddle from the stall railing and set it on a hay bale.

Chance grinned and rolled closer. "Not much of a horse."

"But it's a start. The way I figure it, you can use the stall rungs to pull yourself up and on. Once you're settled, we'll try the bungee straps. This way, you can build up the muscles necessary for the real deal."

"You saying I'm a wimp?"

"Well…"

They both laughed. The once fit and buff Chance was regaining muscle and strength, but he had a ways to go.

They were in the horse barn with an inside arena, something they didn't require today. For now, one of the stalls would do, and the walls both confined them to a safer area and offered slatted railing so Chance could get a handhold. Ace had swept the concrete floor clean to accommodate the wheelchair. He'd also secured the saddle to prevent tipping, running enough wires through the hay to fence a mile section. He couldn't afford to get Chance hurt this early in the game. Or any other time for that matter.

He gestured toward the saddle. "Let's do this."

It took some maneuvering and a few trial runs before they figured the best and easiest way to get Chance onto the saddle, but eventually, they succeeded.

Chance's whoop of accomplishment was worth every effort. He sat for a while to find his balance, but his legs were too long and dragged the floor. "This feels unnatural. I want to get on a horse."

"Now?" The relative safety of the low hay bale was the whole point.

"This was too easy. Look at my legs."

The man had a point. Chance's legs were bent backward at an awkward angle. Finding saddle-worthy balance was nearly impossible. Maybe this wasn't such a grand idea after all.

"We don't want to move too fast." Marisa would kill them both. "You don't have a seatbelt attachment yet or proper straps to secure your legs."

"Don't coddle me, Ace. I get enough of that from my sister. All I'm asking is to sit on a horse for a few minutes, not run in the Kentucky derby. I can hang on to the saddle horn."

Since he put it that way...Should be safe enough. "I'll get Dolly, and we'll see how it goes."

Dolly was one of the ranch's kid ponies. She was bombproof. Nothing rattled her. Chance would be safe on the sweet mare.

He brought Dolly into the barn, and Chance spent a few minutes brushing her red coat while Ace ran his hands over the animal's head and sides and backside. He took some extra time to introduce the docile animal to the wheelchair. With usual horse curiosity, she snuffled at it and then stood quietly as if to say, "What's the big deal?"

Ace's confidence grew. Dolly could handle this.

He saddled the mare and turned her aside to make room for Chance to reach the slats in the stall wall.

"Sure you're ready?"

"Yep." Straining the newly forming arm muscles, Chance slowly pulled himself up the stall. Ace ached to help but knew better than to do anything other than stand close and make sure his pal didn't fall.

When he'd gained the top rail and perched there, legs dangling but hands holding firm, Chance sucked in a winded breath. "Harder than I expected."

"But you did it. The rest should be easy."

Having been ridden by kids, Dolly had been rail-mounted most of her life and offered no objection when Ace led her close to the stall wall.

With less effort that he'd needed to climb the railing, Chance grasped his left knee in both hands and tossed his leg over the saddle, reached for the saddle horn and pulled himself aboard.

Working quickly, Ace ran a bungee cord around each of Chance's legs, securing him to the saddle as much as possible. The lack of special-made straps made him anxious.

"You all right up there? Balanced and set?"

"Feels good. Lead her around the stall."

"Not a good idea."

"Do it, Ace. I'm balanced, and we're in the stall, not the arena."

Ace shot him an exasperated look. "You're a wild man, you know that?"

"Takes one to know one."

"Not anymore. And don't let Marisa hear you say that." With one hand on the mare's neck, he slowly walked her forward a couple of steps. "How's that?"

"Great." Chance sat up straighter, perfecting the rider's posture, though he kept both hands on the saddle horn. "Got a question for you, Ace. Are you in love with my sister?"

Ace carefully allowed the mare a few more steps. "Nosey, aren't you?"

"I need to know the truth. No bull. I don't want her hurt."

"I don't either."

"So, are you?"

Ace sucked in the scent of straw and horse flesh, exhaling in one big gust. "Crazy about her."

"Cool." Chance's voice grew serious. "Are you going to marry her?"

"We haven't gotten that far. Right now, I want her to trust me again."

"She does, or we wouldn't be out here now." Chance leaned forward and patted the mare's neck. At the same time, the mare rounded the stall's corner. Chance's body slipped sideways.

Ace dropped the reins and lunged for his friend's helpless leg. The bungee cord stretched. Chance slid farther to the side, his top-heavy body giving in to gravity. He slammed against the stall wall.

Ace's heart jumped from his chest to his throat. He thought it might choke him to death. If Chance got hurt, he'd wish it had. Grabbing his friend by the arms, he helped him slide to the concrete floor, and leaned them both against the wall.

His pulse rate was at least one-ninety. His breath came in short puffs. "Are you hurt?"

"Just mad." Chance's breath was short too, his face red. "Get me back up there."

"Not tonight, buddy. This lesson is over until we have proper gear." Ace tipped his head back against the wooden stall and patted his chest. "My heart can't take it."

Chance swiveled toward him. "Don't tell Marisa."

Right. Marisa. She'd be livid. Ace lifted his friend's arm to survey the damage. "You may have bruises."

"The worst are probably on my side. It smarts a little. She won't see them."

"I sure hope not."

Ace was beginning to earn her trust again. He couldn't bear to lose it now.

ELEVEN O'CLOCK HAD TAKEN a year to get here.

Marisa, still high on the morning spent with Ace, aimed her Toyota toward the Triple C. Toward home.

He would already be asleep when she arrived. So would Chance. But she liked knowing both the men she loved were nearby.

Something sweet and peaceful had settled inside her at the Sanctuary. Maybe it was the place and knowing the love that had gone into both the reserve and the chapel, but Ace had a lot to do with her new serenity.

As she drove through Clay City, she glanced at her gas gauge, saw it was in the red and pulled into the Kwik-Pic. She was still embarrassed from the last time she'd run out. She wouldn't do that again. For once, she had the money to fill up.

Again, thanks to Ace. Without the guest house, she wasn't sure where she'd have gone or what would've happened to Chance.

The convenience store was quiet. One car pulled away as she slid her debit card into the slot. Inside, the clerk watched her from the counter. Marisa lifted a hand. He responded in kind and turned away. She'd been here lots of times, and he apparently recognized her.

As she held the nozzle and waited for the tank to fill, a pink Jeep pulled up to the opposite pump. Kristin Fairchild got out, showed no interest in the gas pumps, and instead, walked toward Marisa.

Tall and beautiful and dressed in a sleek red sheath and mile-high heels, Kristin must have come from some kind of event.

"Aren't you Marisa Foreman?"

"I'm surprised you remember me."

"We have a mutual friend." Kristin laughed and tossed miles of shampoo-ad hair. "Only, he's more than a friend to me, which you probably know since you're living in his guest house."

Marisa watched the numbers *tick-tick* on the gas pump. More than a friend? What did Kristin mean?

"How do you know about my living arrangements?"

"From Ace, of course, when he explained why he's been so busy. He told me about you and your crippled brother and about how he feels so sorry for both of you. That's why he invited you to his place. Well, that and the awful guilt."

Marisa tried to focus on the gas pump and pretend the other woman's words didn't bother her all. Would the tank ever get full?

"I don't believe he said such a thing."

Kristin pressed manicured fingernails to her lips and pretended regret. "Oh, my. I can see by your shocked expression, you thought he'd moved you to his ranch out of love. You've fallen for him. You poor thing. Honey, I am so sorry. As one woman to another, I must warn you. Ace is not the settling kind."

Hands beginning to shake with the urge to slap a certain beautiful face, Marisa yanked the nozzle from the tank and slammed it back on the hook and jumped in the car.

She roared away, aware she hadn't closed her gas cap and not even caring.

Nothing like meeting one of Ace's old girlfriends to ruin a perfectly wonderful day. And to plant seeds of doubts where trust was trying to grow.

CHAPTER 15

A telephone mooing after midnight could *not* be good news.

Ace rolled to his side and glared at the lighted cell phone. A name and number flashed with the pulsing moo. Don's. His AA mentee.

He grabbed for the cell, sliding the locked screen as he fell back against the pillows. "Hello."

Background noise garbled the voice. Or else someone on the other end was having a hard time forming words. Maybe both.

Ace heard fumbling sounds, a curse, and then what sounded like ice rattling against glass.

"Don? Is that you?"

The noise stopped. The caller sighed. "Yeah. It's me."

The words were slurred.

Ace sat up, the low sinking in his belly almost painful. "What's going on, pal?"

"I messed up."

"Where are you?"

"Not sure. Somewhere. Hey, man," he called to someone else. "What iz zis place?"

Voices Ace couldn't quite decipher answered. Don rattled off the name of Richard's Bar. Ace couldn't recall it, a mercy considering all the bars he'd frequented after the accident.

"In Clay City?"

"I think. Yeah, that's right. Clay City." The sentence ended on a drunken sob. "I messed up. I messed up. Joanie hates me."

"Stay put, Don. I'm on my way."

Leaving the call open, Ace dressed in record time, shoved his feet into his boots, grabbed his keys and headed for his truck.

Don had been doing so well. What had happened?

MARISA HEARD a car motor rumble to life and folded the book she'd been reading against her chest. Who was coming or going on the ranch at this hour? And why?

She closed the book and put it on the nightstand. If not for this page-turner romance novel, she'd have been asleep hours ago.

The vehicle rumbled louder. Curious, she threw the sheet back and padded to the window. Ace's black truck, visible beneath the security light, slid past the guest house and disappeared down the long driveway.

Where was he going at this time of night?

The incident at the gas pumps returned in full-blown living color. Suspicion sprouted like weeds. Had Kristin called him? Was he meeting her somewhere for a secret, late-night tryst?

Marisa remained at the window for a long time, fighting the knot in her stomach, wanting to believe in him. He'd never lied to her before. Not even in the worst of times. Had he been lying today when he'd said he cared for her? He'd spoken with such tender conviction that she'd believed, *really* believed, he loved her.

Today had been wonderful. For him, too, she'd thought. Surely, he wouldn't betray her with another woman.

But what if Kristin had told the truth? What if Ace only wanted to make amends for the accident? He needed absolution. He was determined to clear his conscience. Was the guest house, the trip to the Sanctuary and all the other kindnesses his way of paying a debt?

Was Ace, as Kristin claimed, motivated by pity? For Chance? For her? Or was this another case of her terrible insecurities? Her fear of repeating her mother's mistakes.

She wrestled the thoughts until her head throbbed and finally gave up and went back to bed.

Sleep wouldn't come. Behind her eyes, a sixteen-millimeter film of beautiful, confident Kristin juxtaposed with images from the Sanctuary, the care center, the park, and the wonderful dinners at the Caldwell table.

Which Ace was the real one?

Annoyed at herself for thinking the worst, she sat up, turned on the lamp and took out her Bible. She flipped to a random page, her eyes falling on John 14:27.

She'd not been as faithful with her Bible reading or

prayer as she'd once been. She'd been so busy, and somehow God had gotten pushed to the corner.

Finger to the page, she murmured the comforting words of Jesus. "Peace I leave with you, my peace I give unto you: not as the world giveth, give I unto you. Let not your heart be troubled, neither let it be afraid."

She needed that kind of peace tonight. A Jesus peace.

Eyes drifting closed, she prayed. For herself to have more faith. For Ace to be safe and sober. Anything else was his business, not hers, including any relationship he might or might not have with Kristin, though it hurt her to think so.

It occurred to her then that there were plenty of other reasons Ace could have left the ranch tonight. Maybe he'd gone to check on a pregnant cow. Maybe a friend or neighbor was sick. Perhaps Nate or Emily or one of their family members needed him. She should pray that all was well, not believe the worst of the man she claimed to love.

"Thank you for the reminder, Lord."

When the prayer ended, she lay back on the pillow and meditated on the Scripture, seeking God's peace.

She didn't know how much time passed but eventually, she heard the rumble of Ace's truck and went to the door.

She wouldn't sleep the rest of the night unless she knew all was well with him and with his family.

And if she was still a little suspicious, she couldn't help it.

He parked outside the garage and killed the engine. His automatic lights remained on, and the dome light flashed as he opened the door. Wearily, he stepped from the cab and, head down, started toward the back door of the main house.

Though barefoot and in her pajamas, Marisa walked across the moist grass toward him. He must have sensed her presence because he glanced back and saw her. He looked exhausted. And sad.

She crossed the graveled access road, the rocks stabbing her tender soles. "Is everything all right?"

He waved her off. "Fine. Go back to bed."

By now, she'd reached the grassy back yard. Her feet thanked her for the cool softness.

"You look upset."

"I'm okay. Tired. See you tomorrow." He turned to leave.

Suspicions sprang up. He was being evasive, eager to get rid of her. "Ace. Wait."

He paused, shoulders slumped. A heavy emotion emanated from him. She couldn't place it, but she could feel it.

Marisa slid a caring hand up his back. As she did, her nose picked up a familiar scent. Her hand froze, then dropped away in shock.

"You've been drinking."

"No!" He spun around. The smell intensified.

Marisa recoiled. A child of alcoholics knew that stink. Gin. Vodka. One of those. Drunks thought they were odorless, but they were wrong. Ace reeked of alcohol, and beneath the security light, his eyes were glazed and red.

She knew for certain then. Her suspicions were confirmed.

"You're drunk." She backed away, devastated.

He reached for her. "A friend called."

And she knew who. "Kristin?"

He scowled. "Who? Kristin? No."

Why should she believe him? It was probably another lie. Her voice choked. "You promised."

"And I've kept that promise, Marisa. I was with an AA pal. He was having a rough time and..." He reached toward her.

Marisa slapped his hands away. A fire stirred in her, a fire of disappointment and disgust and anger.

After their beautiful day together, when she'd finally had hope again, Ace had betrayed her. He'd been drinking with another drunk.

"Get away from me." Her voice rose, louder now that the fire burned from her belly and escaped her mouth. "You smell like a bar."

He tried again to touch her. "That's because—"

She shoved him back. He stumbled. Probably because he was too drunk to stay upright.

"Don't touch me. You're drunk!"

"I am not drunk!" He took a step. Reached out. "Let me explain."

Tears pushed at the back of her eyes. Furious tears. She backed away. Her feet found the gravel. The sharp pain added fuel to her fire.

"You lied to me. You lied!" She was shouting now. And she was shaking, her knees wobbly and her voice out of control. The anger she'd held against her parents for years gushed out, drowning Ace. "Liar, user, drunk. I can't believe I let you do this to me again!"

"I didn't. An AA pal was having a bad time—"

Enough. She didn't want to hear this. She spun away. "Marisa. Stop. Listen."

But she was past listening. She'd been the fool Kristin said she was. She'd trusted Ace, and he'd betrayed her.

Again.

ACE WATCHED Marisa storm back to the cottage. He could march right over there, pound on the door and insist she listen to the truth, or he could call it a bad night and try again tomorrow.

Tomorrow had to be better. He'd come home from the bar dog tired, frustrated and heart-sick. And badly in need of a shower. Now, he was also discouraged and hurt.

Marisa thought the worst of him. And she'd not cared enough to stop and listen.

He was worn slick from trying to prove himself. Either she believed in him or she didn't.

"Apparently, she doesn't." Maybe he should give up, forget about her, move on.

With one last annoyed, wounded huff, he dragged himself into the house, taking care not to wake Connie. He'd been a master at sneaking in during his boozing days and had no problem now.

At least, that was his thinking until the next morning at breakfast.

He wandered into the kitchen at six, blurry-eyed but with a work agenda as long as his arm. No shirking today.

He poured himself a cup of Connie's excellent coffee and sipped, burning his tongue. The boss-lady of the house was nowhere to be seen, so he pulled pancake fixings from the cabinets and started the batter.

Connie sailed into the room, her black hair slicked back into a tail, and bumped him out of the way. "Sit. This is my job."

"I can make pancakes."

"Sit." From the fridge, she gathered the fixings for breakfast as she did every morning. The bunkhouse hands would arrive soon, along with Gilbert and any Caldwell who woke up in time.

Ace pulled a chair from the bar and sat, observing her staccato movements, her unusual silence. "Something wrong?"

She shot him a quick glance. "I should ask you."

"Nothing wrong with me. A little tired." He took a long whiff of his coffee cup. Just smelling the caffeine cleared out some of the fog.

"You and Marisa had a big fight last night."

His head popped up. "You heard us?"

"*Sí.* Oh, yes." Connie beat the pancake batter with particular vehemence. "The two of you shout loud enough to wake the neighbors."

Ace sipped at his coffee and, feeling ornery, said, "We don't have neighbors."

"*Exactamente.*" Connie angled toward him, spatula aloft. "Marisa said you are drunk."

"You gonna whack me with that spatula?"

"If you were drinking? *Sí.* Maybe with a pan, too."

"I wasn't." He explained the situation. "I'm a mentor, Connie, a sponsor, we call it in AA. I have a responsibility to Don. He called. I went to the bar and carted his drunk carcass to his apartment, hid his keys, and left. End of story."

She dropped the spatula back in the bowl and crossed the room to touch his hair. A faded memory came, shimmering and gossamer, but as real and sweet as the woman who'd raised him. When he was small, crying for his mama, she'd stroke his hair and sing to him in Spanish.

"Marisa does not believe this?"

"Do you?"

"*Sí.*"

An ease settled over Ace. He hadn't realized how much he needed someone to take him at his word.

"Apparently, Marisa doesn't. She smelled the liquor and started yelling. Wouldn't give me an opportunity to tell her about the drink Don spilled on me."

"Then, you must go and talk to her right away. Explain."

"I tried." He shook his head. "No matter what I do, she doesn't trust me. And for good reason. After what happened before, with her and with Chance—"

"In the past. Water over the bridge." Over the bridge, under the bridge. Connie sometimes twisted expressions.

She patted the top of his head and returned to her batter, stopping to click on the griddle.

"Not to Marisa. She brings it up over and over again." He clunked the mug on the bar with unnecessary force. "I'm done trying. I thought after yesterday when I took her to the Sanctuary..."

"Ahhh." Connie leveled him with a quiet look. "This is more than making up for past mistakes. You are in love with her."

He twitched a shoulder. "Maybe."

"*Si*. You love her. A Caldwell does not take his woman, or man, to the Sanctuary otherwise. It is not done."

What she said was true. He knew it. Had known it when he'd asked Marisa to go with him. The Sanctuary was sacred ground to a Caldwell. Only family was invited. Did he want Marisa to be his family?

Connie lay slices of bacon on a huge baking sheet and slid it into the oven.

Ace pushed up from the bar and ambled toward her, thankful for this sensible woman who loved him, even at his worst. "Need some help with breakfast?"

She flapped a dismissing hand at him and cracked an egg against a ceramic bowl. "What I want is for my heart-son not to be so hard skulled. You love this girl. And I think she loves you too much. That is her problem. She is afraid, and so she looks for reasons to run away."

"Afraid of me?" He poked a finger at his chest.

"No, *hio mio*. She is afraid of herself, of letting anyone get close enough to hurt her the way her parents did. But you"—she pointed an egg at him—"you are already too close. And Marisa does not know what to do."

Ace considered Connie's theory as he rubbed a thumb and forefinger over his chin. His whiskers scraped. He needed a shave. His face felt as rough as the rest of him, especially his gnawed-up insides.

"I would never intentionally hurt her."

"I know. I know. Behind that orneriness, you have a big, good heart. But Marisa, she is a wounded bird. She needs a strong, loving man to believe in."

"I don't know if I can be that guy. If I'll ever be that to

her. I've failed her in a lot of ways, Connie. Especially the boozing and the accident."

"You are drinking no more. Time will erase her worry."

"I guess it wouldn't hurt to talk to her this morning. I don't smell like vodka, and hopefully, she's had a chance to calm down."

The minute he'd gotten to his room last night, he'd hit the shower, eager to erase the smell. The scent had almost gagged him. A new and welcome turn of events.

Connie flapped a hand toward the back door. "Go now. *Vamoose.* I will save your breakfast."

She was right. He wasn't a quitter. And Marisa was worth the effort.

Ace refilled his cup, added another for Marisa, and let himself out the back way.

At the cottage door, he tapped lightly with the side of his boot. Inside, he heard movement.

"Marisa." He kept his voice low in case Chance still slept.

"Leave me alone, Ace. We're through."

He sighed. "Your coffee's getting cold, and I won't go away until we talk."

Silence was his answer, so he tapped the door with his boot again. "I'm a patient man. Can wait all day. Sure is good coffee."

She yanked the door open. Ace's belly tumbled. Her eyes were red and glassy. Had she been crying? Or was she tired after last night's...whatever it was.

"Peace offering." He held out the coffee. "Connie made it."

She took the cup, but turned around and went back inside, leaving him on the porch with the door open.

He followed her in. "Can we talk?"

She stood at the short kitchen counter, dumping creamer into her cup.

"Nothing to talk about." But she started talking anyway. "When I saw your truck pull away last night, I knew something was wrong. But I never dreamed it was *that*."

The disgusted emphasis on *that* gave him a major clue.

"It wasn't."

"So you say."

He set his coffee on the small bar that divided the living room from the kitchen. Searching for the right words, he said, "Will you let me explain what really happened? Or do you want to believe the worst because you're afraid of being in love with me?"

She spun so fast, she jostled her cup and splashed coffee onto the counter. She opened her mouth to argue, but no words came.

Encouraging, in a funny kind of way.

"Connie says I'm in love with you, too." There. It hadn't killed him to admit it. Sort of.

He wanted her to rush into his arms and proclaim her undying devotion. She didn't. Instead, she rolled her eyes with such annoyance, her pupils disappeared. "Oh, that's rich. Like I believe *that*."

He shouldn't have bragged about his patience. She was testing it out big time.

With an exasperated sigh, Ace tugged a chair up to the

bar close to where she stood, and pointed. "Please? Sit, sip your coffee, and listen?"

When she glanced at the chair and hesitated, he held up a hand. "One conversation. Five minutes. Then, if you want to boot me out, I'll go. I'll hate it, but I'll go and never bother you again. What do you have to lose?"

With a backward glance at the spilled coffee, she did as he asked, except she scooted the chair a good three feet away from him.

Back to the cold shoulder. Frost from those chilly gray eyes could send a man to the ER. He could feel the breeze from here.

She crossed her arms and glared at him.

She was acting tough. Protecting herself. Connie's words ran through his head. Marisa was scared.

"You don't have to be afraid of me. I'm not that guy."

"Then why did you stink like the inside of a bottle?"

"I'm a sponsor for another guy in AA who's not as far down the road as I am. He called me from a bar, in bad shape. He fell off the wagon last night." More like, he fell under it and got run over. Twice.

Marisa's eyes remained suspicious, but she was listening. "You went to a bar?"

Slowly, Ace nodded. "I won't lie to you. I did. But not to drink. Fact is, I was nervous that I might be tempted."

"Then why did you go?"

"Because that's what we do. My sponsor was there for me when I was struggling. He never had to haul me out of a bar drunk, but he could have. Alcoholics help each other stay sober."

"But your friend wasn't sober."

"No. He wasn't. His soon to be ex-wife had dinner with another guy. He saw them together, and it was more than he could handle." Ace squeezed a hand over his face. "As much as I wish he'd called me first, he didn't."

"But he was already drunk. Why bother to call? Did he want a drinking buddy?"

"That's not the way it works. He knew I wouldn't. That's why he called. All I did was take him home and make sure he was safe." This morning's hangover would be a killer, the regrets even worse. "He'll hate himself when he wakes up."

Marisa uncrossed her arms. A good sign. "I don't understand why you smelled so strong of vodka. Or whatever the booze *du jour.*"

She had a good nose for strong drink, a shame, but not a surprise considering her background.

"He was so drunk by the time I got there, he resisted my help. Didn't want to leave the bar. We...tussled a bit." Actually, Ace dumped the guy over his shoulder and carted him to the truck.

"He spilled the drink on you?"

"That's the size of it. Cussed me out, too. Threatened to kick my..." He stopped. "You get the picture."

Marisa dipped her head and stared at her hands. She was calm now, really listening.

Ace's heart thudded painfully against his ribs. He was scared too. Scared she wouldn't believe him. Scared of losing her. Scared of failing her and Chance and himself all over again.

"That's all I got, Marisa." He found her eyes, pleaded with his own. "I need you to believe in me."

She stared for a few long seconds, her expression anguished, before her gaze slid away. Hands in her lap, she twisted her fingers, breathed out a long sigh.

Ace felt it then, the change in the air, the resignation that spelled doom. He tried to brace against the inevitable.

Her voice, when it came, was a whisper. "I want to, but I don't know if I can."

The words stabbed deep.

Without trust, they would never work. He knew even if she didn't. They might as well walk away now while they could do it with grace and affection.

Slowly, wearily, Ace nodded.

Nothing he said or did would make any difference. It was the insanity thing again. He kept doing the same things with Marisa, expecting different results, but nothing had changed except her location.

"I understand. I don't blame you." But his heart hurt so badly, he wasn't sure he could get his next breath. "This is it, I guess. The end of you and me."

"I need some time."

She needed time. She needed space. It wasn't him, it was her. Weren't those the words women used to let a man down easy? Famous words of breaking up.

He mocked himself. Breaking up? They'd barely gotten started.

Marisa said no more, but her eyes glistened. Ace waited, let two beats pass and then three, hoping against the odds that she'd say something to give him hope, to offer a reason for him to keep trying.

She didn't.

Trust. Such a simple word and, yet, the most difficult

concept for the woman he loved to internalize. Had she ever trusted anyone?

Maybe not. Maybe she never would. Especially him.

Not her fault. He couldn't even be angry.

He picked up his hat, squeezed the brim between thumb and forefinger. "You're welcome to use the guest house as long as you need or want."

And before he made a fool of himself, Ace exited the cottage, closing the door quietly behind him.

arisa's feet seemed stuck to the floor. She wanted to run after Ace and promise to always believe in him. But that would be a lie. She'd doubted him, accused him, and she wasn't sure she could ever trust anyone. People failed her. People let her down. People hurt her.

What had happened to her Jesus-peace?

Suddenly the door of Chance's room burst open and the wheelchair clattered into the hallway.

A moment later, Chance rolled up to the bar faster than she'd ever seen him move. "Are you completely nuts?"

Marisa slashed a hand across her face. She wasn't crying. She wouldn't cry. "What are you talking about?"

"This is a small house, in case you hadn't noticed." He stabbed a thumb over his shoulder. "I can hear every word in there in my bedroom. I tried to be discreet, but this is ridiculous."

"I'm sorry you overheard. And what's that bruise on your arm?" She jumped up from her chair and rushed to his side.

He shook her off. "I fell off a horse."

"He put you on a horse?" Anger stung through her nerves. "You could have been killed. What was Ace thinking—"

"Leave Ace out of it." Chance cut her off, his handsome face stern. "Getting on the horse was my idea. I insisted, and I'm man enough to make my own decisions. I don't need you or Ace to make them for me. Get that through your head. Stop babying me. I can't take it anymore."

Marisa blinked at her sandy-haired brother, stunned by his vehemence. "What are you so fired up about this morning?"

"You. Ace. This whole ordeal. I'm going to ride a horse, Marisa. And drive and get a job. I have a life to lead and so do you. Stop smothering me. I'm a grown man, not your eleven-year-old kid brother."

"But you're—"

"Paralyzed? Yeah, I am. And I'm dealing with it. It's time for you to deal with it too. I can make the best of it, like Ace says, or I can wallow in self-pity and let my big sister turn herself into a martyr over me the rest of my life."

Marisa stiffened. "I'm not martyring myself."

"Aren't you?"

"No! You're my brother, my responsibility."

"That's where you're wrong." He extended his palms, pleading. "Sis, hear me. You're the best big sister in the world. You've given up everything for me. But that ends today. From this moment on, I'm *my* responsibility."

What had come over him this morning? She placed a hand on his forehead. "Do you have fever?"

Chance laughed, but not a happy sound, and ducked to one side. "You are as hardheaded as that cowboy of yours."

"He's not mine."

"More wrong thinking on your part. You've got to clear out the brain cells. Ace came over here this morning with his heart in his hands. He offered it to you. And you tossed it in his face."

"If you heard that, you heard the rest."

"Yeah. You accused him of partying it up with some AA buddy." He made a *sheeshing* sound and shook his head. "Pathetic."

"We don't know that he wasn't."

"Then, you're hopeless, and you deserve to lose him."

"Chance!" She stared at her brother in wide-eyed hurt. "Are you taking Ace's side against mine?"

"There are no sides. Ace is crazy for you. He told me so last night when he was arguing against me getting on that horse without proper gear."

"He did?"

"Yeah. Now, I got one more thing to say before I go back in that room and take a shower. Without your help."

"Okaaay." She was almost afraid to hear anything else.

"You've never trusted anyone in your life. Not even me."

"That's not true." But it was. She hadn't even trusted Chance to make his own adult decisions.

"Ace is a good man, not perfect, but he's trying hard,

and he loves you so much that he basically blackmailed you into moving out here where he could be close to you. He wanted you to see him in action every day. To be with you during down times. To have breakfast and Sunday dinner with you. To show you the kind of good man he really is. To make you laugh again."

"Did he tell you that?"

"Yeah. We talk about stuff. He's breaking his back to give you reasons to trust him again, to forgive him and to love him." He rolled his chair away from the bar. "You gotta stop being scared, Sis. Let it go. Ace isn't Mom or Dad. He's not even the Ace we knew before. He's better. Open your eyes and accept what he's freely offering before it's too late."

"I don't know if I can." The same words she'd said to Ace when he'd pleaded with her to trust him.

"You can do anything. Just open that heart of yours and take the risk. You won't be sorry." He spun the chair around and started back to his room. Over one shoulder, he called, "Hold on, I want to read something to you."

Puzzled, pensive, Marisa refilled her coffee and, out of long habit, poured a cup for her brother.

He returned with a Bible in his lap. "I was reading this the other night and it reminded me of someone."

"What is it?"

"Corinthians 13. Listen up." He glanced down and then up again. "Talking about love. God's kind."

Marisa listened in amazement. Chance had been turned off to God since before the accident. Was this Ace's influence too?

"Love does not dishonor others, it is not self-seeking,

it is not easily angered, it keeps no record of wrongs." He glanced up when he read that part, and his navy-blue eyes nailed her.

She'd been guilty of remembering wrongs. Especially against Ace. She'd been focused on herself. Not on Chance, though that's what she'd told herself. Yes, she'd wanted to protect him, but she'd only made things worse. And this time, Ace hadn't been selfish at all. Everything he'd done had been for her and Chance.

"Listen to this part." Her brother continued reading in his baritone voice. Not a boy's voice. A man's. "Love always protects, always trusts, always hopes, always perseveres." He put his fingers on the thin paper. "Sounds like someone we know, doesn't it?"

"Yes." And she'd been the total opposite. While Ace had been protecting, trusting, hoping and persevering, she'd fought against him with her doubt and fear.

But he hadn't given up. Until today.

All she had to do was look at the positive changes in her brother to see the good in Ace Caldwell. All she had to do was stop expecting the worst and choose to trust. A choice.

Something shifted inside of Marisa, like an iceberg jostled loose. Blinders placed there by years of bad experience suddenly fell away.

Her pulse clattered against the side of her neck. "I wonder if he's still at the house."

"One way to find out."

She needed no other encouragement.

As she flew across the gravel road, the back door to the main house opened and her cowboy exited. With long, strong strides, Ace met her halfway. She reached for him. He never even questioned. He simply pulled her into his embrace and rocked her back and forth, back and forth. He gripped her with such restrained strength, his arms quivered, and she felt cherished.

He'd taken her in, no questions asked, no recriminations. Oh, she loved this man. What a fool she'd been!

A firestorm of emotion erupted from her throat. "I'm sorry. I trust you. I love you. How did you know?"

His laugh was soft against her hair. "Chance texted. Said you were headed my way."

"I love that boy. I mean, man."

"Me, too. In a brotherly kind of way." And they both laughed.

"Can you forgive me for being so stupid?" she asked.

"Already have. Can you forgive me?" Still holding her as if afraid to let go, he gently moved her away so they were face to face, heart to heart. His serious green eyes bore into her, pleading. He was desperate for her forgiveness, her love, her trust.

She'd hurt this good man. But never again.

Marisa didn't know what had happened or at what point she'd let go of their ugly past, but as she searched her heart, she discovered the truth. "Love doesn't remember wrongs. And it always trusts."

"And protects. Let me protect you and love you, Marisa. Can you trust me to do that?"

Fear tried to raise its ugly head. *What if—* Marisa stopped the thought half-formed. No more what-ifs. No more mistrust. "I do. I will. And if I ever get crazy again, do something drastic."

"Like this?" His beloved face moved closer until their lips met in a short, sweet kiss.

Marisa smiled. "Not drastic enough."

She pulled him back for another kiss, this one longer and filled with all the love and trust she could give.

When the moment ended, she didn't let go, didn't step away. She stroked the sides of his face the way he'd done for her so many times. His eyes sparkled, happy and loving, but they were tired too. Not hung-over, as she'd thought. The eyes of a man sacrificing his rest to do a good deed.

"I have a question for you." She pressed her lips against the corner of his mouth.

"Keep doing that and I'll tell you anything." His hands rubbed up and down her back, distracting her, but she didn't want him to stop.

"Just one." She kissed the other corner.

"And it is?"

Her heart ricocheted against her ribs. "Am I really the only person you've ever taken to the Sanctuary?"

"You are."

"Why?"

"You know why. I'm in love with you. The way my dad loved my mom. Someday, when you're ready, I want to marry you."

She tilted her head, heart singing. "Are you saying you'll wait for me?"

"I tried breaking up with you for about thirty minutes this morning. I hated it."

"So did I. Let's don't do that anymore."

"Deal."

In the pastures, cows mooed for their babies. The morning ebbed around the two people standing between the guest house and the Triple C Ranch house. Truck doors slammed. Voices lifted on the barely breeze. Family coming home for breakfast, though Marisa knew now that family came in all shapes, sizes and colors and didn't have to share blood to share love.

Ace had brought her here, had known what she needed even when she'd fought against it. Home. Family. Him.

"Breakfast is ready," he said. "Will you come in?"

A loaded question. She'd been on the outside looking for too long. Today, as Chance insisted, all of that would change.

Full of joy and release, she slid her arm around the lean waist of her cowboy and began the journey toward her future.

EPILOGUE

The engagement of Ace Caldwell to Marisa Foreman surprised exactly no one who knew them. The real surprise came when they waited a year to tie the knot.

But today was the day. Marisa Foreman had joined her life to Ace Caldwell, the man she'd been afraid to hope for. She glanced at her left hand, admiring the wedding ring Ace had slid on her finger, his voice strong and sure as he'd pledged to love and cherish her all the days of her life.

A girl could swoon at hearing words like that from the man she adored.

He stood next to her now, at their reception here at the Calypso Country Club, hand at her waist as if he couldn't stop touching her. She knew how he felt. Today, he was hers in a new way, and they could touch all they wanted.

Her handsome cowboy looked especially resplendent

in a western tux of black jacket, dark jeans and shiny black boots. He made her heart flutter. Dance. Sing. All the mushy clichés she'd read in romance novels. Above the white shirt and silver vest, his green eyes glowed, and she knew the look was for her alone.

Ace's warm breath brushed against her ear. "Hey, beautiful, the photographer wants you to kiss me. Anyway, I think it was the photographer's idea. Might have been mine."

"Brilliant you or brilliant photographer." Pink bouquet in hand, she put her arms over his shoulders and kissed him. If the kiss went on longer than necessary for a few dozen good photos, neither of them minded. This is where they both belonged.

Ace had given her the time she needed to grow as a woman, as a believer, and to work through the issues that held her bound, and she'd given him time to grow stronger in his sobriety. They'd spent weeks with the pastor in premarital counseling, learning how to be the best mates possible. They'd done it together, side by side, encouraging and loving every step. When Ace had received his two-year sobriety coin, they'd celebrated with a fancy dinner and a concert in Tulsa. Her treat. Now, he was approaching year three. She was proud of him, and very, very proud to be his lady.

She'd also refused to burden Ace with her debts, but now that Chance was teaching again, he'd taken on much of the responsibility. If the hospital bills were far lower than she'd expected, Ace wouldn't admit to being responsible. God, he'd reminded her, worked in mysterious ways, and if God chose to reduce Chance's medical bills, who was she to argue?

He was so good to her. Good to her brother, too.

Looking back, she was thankful that Ace had refused to take no for an answer. He'd pushed and persisted and persevered, and in the doing, had given Chance his life back. Her too.

She'd been blinded by her lousy childhood.

Chance still had his struggles, but he was thriving, forging ahead with a future she'd never dreamed possible. He'd taken a few classes to certify in other teaching areas besides coaching and had landed a job teaching math at Calypso High.

She glanced at her brother, handsome in his wheelchair, wearing a dark suit and white shirt, his pink tie matching her wedding colors of pink and silver. His white teeth flashed at something a pretty young woman said. She'd come to the wedding at Chance's invitation, a good sign that her brother still wielded a powerful attraction to the ladies.

Beside her, Ace fidgeted and, in a low, sexy growl, murmured in her ear, "I'm ready to get out of here."

The former party animal was eager to ditch the party. So was she. The rest of the Caldwells would feast and dance and celebrate all day. Mr. and Mrs. Ace had a plane to catch. Later. First, Marisa had a surprise for him. She was a little nervous, but excited too. Emily said the plan was perfect.

"Let's say our goodbyes and go now," she said.

"See why I married you? You have the best ideas."

She hoped he'd think the next one was even better.

He took her hand and started the rounds.

The morning wedding had been simple, beautiful and private, the way they both wanted. The reception was something else. Marisa thought half the county must be crowded into the country club ballroom.

When they'd done their best to meet and greet and offer food, drink and an afternoon of entertainment to the guests, they slipped out the side door.

On approaching his black truck, Ace froze and perched both fists on his hips. "Add another stop at the car wash."

She laughed. "I like it."

Someone had decorated the vehicle with happy faces, kissing lips, funny advice, and pink balloons. A *Just Married* sign dangled from the tailgate.

"Come to think of it, so do I. I want the whole world to know you finally married me." Keys in hand, he pressed the remote and unlocked.

Marisa made her move, scooting in between him and the door. She held her hand out for the keys. "Go around, cowboy, I'm driving."

"No, you're not."

"Are we going to have our first fight on our wedding day?" She cocked her head, smiling when she said it.

"Why?"

"Because I have a surprise for you. Please. With sugar on top."

He released the keys. "Never could resist a surprise. Or sugar."

He smooched her forehead and jogged to the passenger side.

She slid into the driver's seat and drove them toward the Triple C. Ace held her hand across the console and muttered about how much he missed bench seats. So did she. She'd love to be snuggled at his side.

They talked about the wedding, the guests who'd come, the beautiful array of gifts, but mostly, they gloated in the moment.

They passed the big house where they would live after the honeymoon. Ace shot her a questioning look but she only smiled and kept her secret. She was excited and a little nervous but desperate to give something special and memorable to the man who'd done so much for her.

When they reached the entrance to the white gate bearing the Triple C brand, Ace turned toward her, his expression soft. "The Sanctuary."

"Do you mind?"

In answer, he got out and opened the gate and then rejoined her in the truck. She drove them deeper into the preserve, parking where he'd parked that first time more than a year before. They exited the vehicle, and Marisa stood beside her husband in the sun-speckled copse of trees, breathing in the hallowed, floral-scented air.

Like the first time, birds dipped and darted amidst the trees while others serenaded the quiet.

They didn't speak. The moment seemed too special, too holy. It was a beautiful thing to be one with this man who understood her like no other. He would know why they were here.

Smiling, she took his hand and led him toward the chapel and the place where his parents had been laid to rest.

She stopped beside the gravestone and crouched to place her bouquet there.

"Mr. and Mrs. Caldwell, today I married your son, and I've come to ask your blessing." The white doves, cast in eternal devotion, stared back at her as if listening. "I wish you were here to see what a wonderful man he is, and I want you to know how loved he will be by his new wife."

She glanced up at her husband, and his glassy eyes touched a place in her heart. He was touched, too, and pleased.

Ace went to a knee beside her and clutched her hand. "Mom and Dad, I love this woman. She means the world to me. That she would plan to bring me here on our wedding day shows you what kind of woman she is. Mom, she's a lot like you, I think, generous, kind-hearted and independent. When she loves, she means it. So do I." He reached out, traced his father's name. "Dad, if I can be half the man you were…"

Marisa put her fingers over his. "You are. Oh, my husband, you are."

For several moments, they remained kneeling, contemplative and prayerful though not in a formal way. When Marisa rose, Ace rose with her. They turned to face each other. As they'd done in the church earlier that day, they joined hands.

Marisa, chest bursting with joy and love, spoke first, letting out the private words meant only for him.

"I don't have riches to bring to this marriage, but I give you what I have. My heart. My loyalty. My future. This moment here in this special place with your parents…" Her eyes drifted to the white doves, then back to her handsome husband. "Today, in front of your parents, on this holy ground, I embrace you and all that your family stands for. Your traditions, your faith, the things that matter to you. I freely, joyfully, totally commit everything I am to you."

Ace brought her hands to his mouth and kissed each knuckle. Her whole body tingled from the tenderness. His gaze, green as the elm leaves, held hers while he spoke.

"And I freely share everything with you, Mrs. Caldwell, and embrace all that is you. Beautiful, warm-hearted, generous you. You make me better, make me want to be the man I see in your eyes. Thank you for this. I can't begin to express what coming to the Sanctuary on this day means to me. But you knew." He kissed her gently, sweetly. "You knew this would mean more than all the fancy weddings in the world. I love you even more because of it."

That was exactly what she'd planned. To see him fulfilled, the way he'd fulfilled her.

"Once, in this very place, you said you wanted the kind of love your parents had. I promise that to you, my Ace of hearts. I will be the wife you need and want, devoted forever and beyond."

"And I promise the same to you with my parents as our witnesses."

"I think they know, don't you?"

"Oh, yes. They know. I feel them here."

He gave a contented sigh and turned them toward the stone. The white doves, faithful and true, seemed to smile, and Marisa was sure she heard the quiet whisper of heavenly blessing.

ABOUT THE AUTHOR

Winner of the RITA Award for excellence in inspirational fiction, Linda Goodnight has also won the Booksellers' Best, ACFW Book of the Year, and a Reviewers' Choice Award from Romantic Times Magazine. Linda is a New York Times bestselling author.

Linda has appeared on the Christian bestseller list and her romance novels have been translated into more than a dozen languages. Active in orphan ministry, this former nurse and teacher enjoys writing fiction that carries a message of hope and light in a sometimes dark world.

She and husband Gene live in Oklahoma with their daughters.

www.lindagoodnight.com

ALSO BY LINDA GOODNIGHT

TRIPLE C COWBOYS

Twins for the Cowboy

A Baby for the Cowboy

A Bride for the Cowboy

HONEY RIDGE

The Memory House

The Rain Sparrow

The Innkeeper's Sister

THE BUCHANONS

Cowboy Under the Mistletoe

The Christmas Family

Lone Star Dad

Lone Star Bachelor

WHISPER FALLS

Rancher's Refuge

Baby in His Arms

Sugarplum Homecoming

The Lawman's Honor

REDEMPTION RIVER

Finding Her Way Home

The Wedding Garden

A Place to Belong

The Christmas Child

The Last Bridge Home

THE BROTHERS' BOND

A Season for Grace

A Touch of Grace

The Heart of Grace

Made in the USA
Middletown, DE
21 November 2017